"You need a little educating," he taunted.

She swallowed, once again shockingly aware of the message his body was sending out. "That depends on what kind of education you have in mind."

He smiled wickedly as his mouth brushed over her eyelids, closing them. "Nothing traumatic," he murmured. "Just some remedial lovemaking."

Before she could find an answer to that blatant observation, his mouth was on hers. She stiffened for an instant at the intimacy. But as the pressure began to deepen, she felt a hunger, a need, flash like brushfire throughout her being....

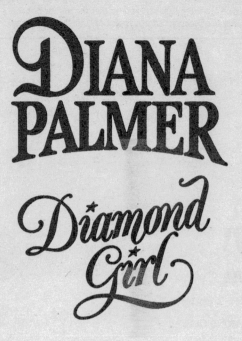

DIANA PALMER

Diamond Girl

MIRA BOOKS

MIRA

ISBN 1-55166-149-7

DIAMOND GIRL

Copyright © 1984 by Diana Palmer.

All rights reserved. Except for use in any review, the reproduction or utilization of this work in whole or in part in any form by any electronic, mechanical or other means, now known or hereafter invented, including xerography, photocopying and recording, or in any information storage or retrieval system, is forbidden without the written permission of the publisher, MIRA Books, 225 Duncan Mill Road, Don Mills, Ontario, Canada M3B 3K9.

All characters in this book have no existence outside the imagination of the author and have no relation whatsoever to anyone bearing the same name or names. They are not even distantly inspired by any individual known or unknown to the author, and all incidents are pure invention.

MIRA and the star colophon are trademarks of MIRA Books.

Printed in U.S.A.

To Jeanette,
and to the girls at Carwood

Chapter One

It was raining in chilly gray torrents, and Kenna Dean made puddles on the floor beside her desk as she shed her beige raincoat and its matching hat. Even her long, wavy dark hair was soaked, and she pushed it angrily out of her bespectacled eyes. She was already ten minutes late because she'd missed the bus, and now her suede boots were drenched along with the hem of her new blue ruffled frontier skirt. She sighed wearily. What was the use? She had just bought the new frontier skirt and a matching high-necked ruffled blouse on Saturday, and this morning she walked out of her small apartment with confidence. Today she was going to make Denny Cole look at her and see a woman, not just an efficient secretary who made good coffee. But then it rained and she'd missed the bus and had to walk four blocks to the downtown Atlanta law office where she worked. It was starting out to be a typical Monday.

Denny Cole's office door opened just as she had known it would, and her tall, boyishly attractive boss walked into the outer office. One fair eyebrow rose expressively as he looked across at her, and she could see that he was struggling not to laugh. She could imagine how she looked: tall, gangly, and small-breasted, wearing clothes that suddenly seemed to emphasize all the faults in her figure. To complete the image of disaster, her mascara was running down her cheeks. She looked like an ideal applicant for the Ringling Brothers & Barnum and Bailey Circus.

"Go ahead, say it," she dared him, pursing her full lips, which were ineffectually painted with thick, pink lipstick. "I'm off to join the clowns."

"I'm a gentleman, or I might," he admitted, letting his white teeth show in a smile as he jammed his hands into his pockets and moved closer. "What's on the agenda today, Kenna?"

Just like that. No notice of anything except the job, even when she looked horrible. She should have known better than to try to dress up for him.

She reached into the top drawer and pulled out the appointment book. "You've got Mrs. Baker about the property suite at nine, you're due in court at ten-thirty on the James case, and you've got a meeting in chambers with Judge Monroe at two-thirty. Isn't he sitting on the James case?"

He nodded.

"Then if you don't finish by two-thirty, you can forget the meeting in chambers, I suppose."

"Are you kidding?" he chuckled. "Henry will recess until we talk over that continuance. How about the rest of the afternoon?"

"You're free."

"Thank God," he sighed. He winked at her. "I've got a heavy date with Margo tonight. I don't know how I live from evening to evening!"

She tried to smile and look unconcerned, while her heart was being slowly strangled by the thought of the dark-haired, dark-eyed beauty he'd been dating for the past two months. It was beginning to look serious, and she was really scared. How would she live if Denny married someone else? She seemed to have loved him forever—at least for the past year. And all he ever noticed was her typing speed.

"Has Regan come in yet?" he asked.

She felt herself tense at the thought of Denny's older stepbrother. He frightened her with his hard, dark face and his huge physique. He was the most abrasively masculine man she'd ever known, and the six months he'd been in partnership with Denny had been the most trying of her work history. She still couldn't understand why Regan had left a lucrative law practice in New York to come down to Atlanta and join Denny's, when Regan already had a national reputation as a trial lawyer and Denny was just out of law school.

"I don't think so," she murmured after a minute. "I just walked in the door, and I haven't looked."

"You won't, either, unless I insist, will you?" he asked curiously. "It amazes me how nervous you are around my brother. The other day he told me that you seem to go into hiding when he's here. He has to hunt for you to give dictation.''

She shifted restlessly. She wasn't a timid person. She had a temper and on occasion she showed it even to Denny. But Regan made her bristle. She couldn't be in the same room with him for five minutes without wanting to take his trash can and dump it over his shaggy dark head of hair. And that wouldn't do at all because Denny worshipped his brother. So she tried to avoid trouble by avoiding Regan Cole. In her mind they were one and the same.

"I'm busy most of the time," she reminded him. "There are those files in the storeroom that I'm trying to alphabetize when I'm not typing petitions for you or entertaining nervous clients...."

"I know, I know," he sighed. He cocked his head at her, and his fair hair, so unlike Regan's, glinted gold in the fluorescent light. "You don't like Regan, do you?" he asked bluntly.

She shrugged her thin shoulders. "I suppose I'm a little in awe of him," she said after a minute, searching for a tactful way to admit that she hated his guts and finding none.

"Because he's famous?" Denny chuckled. "His name always makes the gossip column when he goes to Hollywood or the Big Apple, all right. Regan attracts women the way honey attracts bees. He's not a bad-looking devil, and, God knows, he's not poor.

"Come to think of it, I'm surprised he didn't bring his own secretary when we began the partnership," Denny murmured, smiling. "Sandy was quite a dish. Uh, not that you aren't..."

She managed a faint smile, to show him that she didn't mind being thought of as drab and uninteresting by the man she worshipped.

"Maybe Sandy didn't want to leave New York," she suggested.

"Maybe." He turned. "Well, send Mrs. Baker in as soon as she gets here. I'm not snowed under with mail yet, am I?"

"I'll run down to the mail room and get it," she said.

"Made coffee?" he called over his shoulder.

Sure, she muttered to herself, and swept the floors and de-cobwebbed the corners and re-upholstered the chairs and the sofa and patched the carpet and painted the door facings, all in the past three minutes since I walked in the door.

"Not yet," she replied sweetly. "As soon as I get back, okay?"

He sighed. "I guess it will have to be," he mumbled, closing his door behind him.

"Oh, damn men everywhere," she muttered as she opened the outer door, and came face to face with Regan Cole.

She had to force herself not to start at the unexpected sight of him. He was intimidating—not only his superior height, but the sheer size of him, and not an ounce of that physique was flab. He could back down most opponents just by standing up. His eyes were brown with amber specks, and they were hard and cold as ice when he was angry. His face was broad, his mouth chiseled and faintly sensuous, his nose was too big and had been broken at least twice; it matched his hands and feet, which were equally oversized. But somehow they all suited him.

She moved quickly aside to let him enter the office, and felt herself bristle as he came by her. He had a frightening vitality, an aura of pure menace when he was out of sorts. And he was always out of sorts with Kenna.

"I'm expecting a letter from a colleague in New York," he said without preamble and without a trace of good humor. "Bring the mail in as soon as you get it."

His broad back disappeared into his office and the door closed behind it. She glared at it and, giving in to a sudden whim, went down on her knees and salaamed in front of his closed door. Just as she was giving her best to the effort, the door suddenly opened again.

Regan's thick eyebrows rose while Kenna struggled to regain both her feet and her forgotten dignity.

"I'll need you for some dictation when you get the mail, so bring your pad in with it," he said curtly.

"And if you're auditioning for the stage, don't practice on my time."

He turned back into his office and slammed the door.

There was a muffled laugh from behind her, and she turned to see Denny struggling to keep a straight face. They looked at each other and burst into laughter, rushing out into the hall together to keep from exploding where Regan could hear them.

This was Denny at his best, a co-conspirator with a sense of humor that she loved. Regan's exact opposite, in every way.

"I thought you were going to faint when he opened the door," Denny chuckled, leaning back against the wall in the deserted corridor as the laughter passed. "That made my morning."

"I wasn't expecting him to open the door," she confessed. "I couldn't help it, he throws orders around like a conquering army."

"He always has. I've learned to nod my head and listen and then go do what I please. It works half the time," he added with a rueful smile. "Poor kid, he's rough on you, I know. I truly didn't realize he was going to leave his own secretary behind in New York and then want to share mine."

She flushed at that unexpected sympathy and smiled up at him. "It's okay," she murmured, ready to wade through crocodile infested waters for him. "I'd better get the mail before his lordship comes out with battle axe in hand. Then I'll get your coffee."

"No rush, I'll survive," he said with a wink. "Don't let him intimidate you, Kenna. He's not what he seems. In a lot of ways, Regan's had a hard life." He straightened away from the wall. "Chin up, and all that rot," he said in his best fake British accent. "Right, troops?"

She saluted. "Aye, sir!" She turned and rushed down to the elevator.

A little over an hour later, she was sitting at her desk when Denny came out, shrugging into his trench coat on the way.

"I'm late again," he sighed and smiled at her. "I should be back by three-thirty. You can call the courthouse if you need me before then."

"Will do," she promised. "Have a nice day."

"I'll do my best. Oh, pull out the Myers file and photostat those deeds for me, will you? And do a cover letter, along the lines of, 'Dear Mr. Anderson, enclosed please find copies of the deeds for the Myers land dispute. When you have looked them over, see if you concur with our client's contention that the new survey confirms his ownership of land his neighbor has deeded for an industrial park. I will wait to hear from you, etc.' Okay?"

She was scribbling on the back of an envelope, because, as usual, he wasn't waiting for her to open her pad. "Got it," she agreed.

"Hold the fort, honey," he called over his shoulder. He stopped with his hand on the doorknob. "Oh, if Margo calls, tell her I'll pick her up at six for the ballet, okay? That's my girl."

And he was gone. She glared at the door, feeling vaguely betrayed. She hated Margo, because Margo was beautiful. The Argentinian woman was black-haired and black-eyed, with a complexion like ivory and the most sensuous figure Kenna had ever seen. She ached to look like that, to have that slinky walk and that air of unshakable confidence that drew men like flies. She got out her compact and stared at the plain little face in the mirror with a rueful smile. She wasn't going to set any men on fire with desire, that was for sure. With a sigh she put away the compact and rolled a sheet of letterhead into the electronic typewriter.

The morning went quickly, and pleasantly. Regan stayed in his office. His clients came and went, and the telephone lines stayed busy, but Kenna didn't have to see him. She liked days like this, when confrontations could be avoided. She didn't like Regan. She didn't exactly know why, but compared to his stepbrother, he was like winter to spring. Denny was so personable and pleasant, such a charming man. The only thing Regan might appear charming to would be something as dangerous as he was—maybe a rattlesnake.

She was grinning wickedly at that thought when Regan's office door opened and he came out into the office with curt, deliberate steps.

"Get me the Myers file," he said curtly.

She had it on the desk, having just photocopied the deeds. He rattled her, though, when he used his courtroom tone on her, and she jumped up and started looking through the filing cabinet for it.

His dark eyes went over her with distaste before they fell to the desk. His big hand moved, lifting the edge of the file folder. "Isn't this it?" he asked, his voice sharp.

She turned, flushing as she realized it was. "Yes, sir," she said for lack of anything more original.

He opened it, thumbing through it. His eyes shot up, pinning hers. "What are you doing with it?"

"Denny dictated a cover letter on his way out," she explained coldly, "and said to copy the deeds and send them along."

He tossed the file back onto her desk with a scowl. "I wish to God he'd take time to tell me when he's already done something he's asked me to do."

"He was in a hurry," she said defensively. "He had to be in court by nine-thirty."

He rammed his hands in his pockets and studied her. She wished she hadn't been standing up; that derisive going-over was embarrassing.

"Seen enough?" she asked, angry at his bold inspection.

"I saw enough the day I walked in the door," he said, turning. "Is he taking that Margo woman out again tonight?"

She felt a surge of pleasure at the disapproval in his voice. He didn't care for Denny going out with Margo either, by the sound of it. "You'll have to ask him that, Mr. Cole," she said demurely.

He gave her a sideways glance. "So protective, Miss Dean," he growled. "Denny's a grown man, he doesn't need a bodyguard."

"Most secretaries are protective of their bosses," she parried.

"You carry it to new heights." His glittering eyes narrowed. "How long have you been here?"

"Almost two years," she said.

"How long have you been in love with my brother?" he continued, and she didn't like the mocking smile that held no trace of amusement.

She felt her muscles contract, every one of them, and her eyes glittered behind the big frames of her glasses. "It's hard to work that long around a man without being fond of him," she countered.

He stuck his big hands in his pockets, obviously enjoying himself. "Are you fond of me?" he returned.

"Oh, just burning up with fondness for you, sir," she replied, and grinned wickedly.

"Is that why you were salaaming at my office door when I came in this morning?" he asked politely.

She felt the flush coming again and averted her face before it showed, pretending to gather up the photostated documents on her desk. "I dropped a pencil. I was picking it up," she informed him.

"The hell you were."

She glanced up at him. "Was there something else, Mr. Cole?" she asked.

"Eager to get rid of me?" he questioned, arching his thick eyebrows. "I wouldn't think a woman of your attributes would turn away male attention."

She was doing a slow burn, but perhaps she was getting angry without reason. "My attributes?"

His dark eyes narrowed as they appraised all of her that was visible over the desk. "Small though they are," he added with pursed lips. "Was that outfit supposed to catch Denny's eye?"

She clenched her jaw. "I beg your pardon?"

"That outfit," he repeated, pulling a hand from his pocket to gesture toward her blouse. "You'd look better in a pair of overalls."

She stood up, seething. "Mr. Cole, you may be one of my employers," she began coldly, "but that gives you no right to criticize the way I dress."

"I have to look at you," he replied. "Surely I have a say in the decor of my own office?"

"This," she indicated her clothing, "is the latest style. Pioneers wore clothes like this," she added with pointed sarcasm.

"No wonder the Indians attacked them," he remarked.

Her fingers clenched. Her lips compressed. She wanted nothing more than to attack *him*.

"If you want to take my brother's eyes away from his Latin acquisition, you'll have to do better than that," he persisted. "You look about twelve in that getup. And what do you do to your hair to make it stand on end like that—watch horror movies before you come to work?"

Her fingers curled around the file folder viciously.

"Are you such a prize, Mr. Cole?" she asked coldly.

"Your nose is too big and so are your feet and you're nobody's idea of Mr. Beautiful!"

His eyebrows arched. "This, from a woman who could qualify for the Frump of the Year nomination?"

"Oh!" she burst out, and before she had time to think, she had flung the file folder at him, scattering paper all over the desk and the floor.

He cocked his head at her, a peculiar smile momentarily softening his hard features. "How fortunate for you that it didn't connect," he murmured. "I hit back, honey."

"You started it!" she accused, her eyes flaming green and brilliant, changing her face so that despite the inadequacy of her makeup, she was almost pretty.

"A matter of opinion." He pulled out a cigarette and lit it calmly, watching her hesitate before she reluctantly bent to pick up the scattered papers.

Her fingers were trembling; her body was trembling. She wanted nothing more than to hurt him, to wound him. She couldn't remember ever feeling such rage at any man.

And especially her boss. She colored, remembering that. He'd be within his rights to fire her, and that would take her right out of Denny's life, because Denny wouldn't go against Regan. She'd seen proof of that often enough.

She glanced up at him apprehensively as she clutched the disordered sheets of paper to her bosom and stood up.

"Feeling apologetic?" he asked, and the cold smile told her he understood exactly why she was regretting her temper.

She swallowed her pride. Any sacrifice, to be near Denny. "I'm very sorry, Mr. Cole," she choked. "It won't happen again."

"Poor little Cinderella," he murmured mockingly, and took a draw from his cigarette while she blushed again. "Sitting among the ashes while the wicked stepsister makes away with the handsome prince."

"Yes, indeed," she returned curtly, "almost as bad as having to kiss the frog." She smiled meaningfully at him.

He turned away. "I wouldn't hold my breath, if I were you," he murmured. "I'm damned particular about who kisses me."

"I'm amazed," she muttered. "You probably have to pay women to do that."

"What was that?" he asked, turning.

In enough trouble already, she controlled her temper. "Not a thing, sir," she replied with a theatrical smile. "Just commenting on the weather."

"It would break your heart if I fired you, wouldn't it?" he asked suddenly, looking disgustingly smug. "Because Denny wouldn't lift a finger to bring you back, and you know it."

"That would be hitting below the belt, counselor," she said quietly.

"Yes, it would. I might remind you," he added with a flash of a mocking smile, "that I'm a criminal lawyer. I don't mind hitting where it hurts the most. Do we understand each other, Miss Dean?"

She swallowed. "Yes, sir, we understand each other."

"One more thing," he said, as he took a step into his office and turned with cold brown eyes to look back at her. "The next time you throw anything at me, you'd better be wearing your track shoes."

And he closed the door behind him.

She spent the rest of the day avoiding him, finding excuse after excuse not to go near his office. She didn't like Regan Cole, but it was even more apparent that he disliked her. He always had, since the day he walked into the office for the first time and saw her. She didn't think she'd ever forget the coldness in his eyes, the instant hostility that had met her tentative greeting. He couldn't have made his dislike more obvious if he'd shouted at her. Not that he minded allowing her to take his dictation and his phone calls and type his briefs, she thought angrily. Oh, no, he didn't mind letting her work herself into a frenzy trying to cope with his impatience and his black temper.

When Denny walked back into the office at three-thirty, she was still simmering.

"Hi, girl." Denny grinned, whistling a gay tune as he sauntered in and perched himself on her desk. "How's it going?"

"You had four calls. I put the messages on your desk. And I've got the letter on the Myers file in there for your signature, complete with copies," she said, warming to his charm. He was like a breath of spring compared to his wintery stepbrother.

"Is Regan in?"

She felt her face go rigid. "He left about a half hour ago."

He cocked his head at her. "You say that with such relish," he murmured, grinning.

"For my part, I wish he was in darkest Africa, being slowly cooked in somebody's stew pot, pith helmet and all," she said, visualizing the scene with glee. "Of course, he'd poison whoever ate him...."

"How savage," he remarked. "Might I ask why you have this sudden compulsion to feed my stepbrother to strangers?"

"He called me a frump," she returned with glittering eyes. "Not only that, he hinted that I was a public eyesore and should be under Indian attack...."

His eyebrows arched toward the ceiling. "He what?"

She cleared her throat. "Well, never mind, it's too complicated," she murmured.

"He doesn't like you, does he, little one?" he asked quietly. "I've noticed how hostile he is toward you. It's not like Regan; he's usually the soul of courtesy with women."

"Ah, but that's the problem," she explained, grinning. "He doesn't think I qualify for the status of a woman. I look about twelve in this rig, he said."

Denny didn't say a word, but his eyes revealed that his own opinion matched his brother's. "Might I ask what you were doing while all this commentary was going on?"

"Flinging file folders at his shaggy head, that's what," she returned. "And if you want to fire me, go ahead."

He chuckled softly, his eyes gleaming with delight.

"Oh, no, lady, not me. If you're brave enough to throw things at Regan, you've got a job for life."

She smiled sheepishly. "Old dragonslayer, that's my name," she murmured. "Not that the dragon didn't flame up," she added with a sigh. "He said if I threw anything else at him, I'd better be good at track."

"I don't doubt it. Take my word for it, Regan in a temper is something to be avoided at all costs."

"I'll keep that in mind as I sharpen my trusty saber."

"Better not rattle it too loudly, either. Want me to talk to him about you?" he asked with genuine concern.

She sighed. "He'd probably chew it up, too," she replied. "Don't talk to him, please. He'll just accuse me of crying on your shoulder and it will only make things worse. I can take care of myself."

"If worse comes to worse, I'll insist that he bring in his own secretary," Denny promised. "Maybe he misses New York after being away six months. I can't imagine why he gave up that practice to come south, although it's sure been great for me. I never would have gotten such a big start without his help.''

"He asked me if you were seeing Margo," she confided.

He frowned. "And what did you tell him?" he asked, his voice cool.

"Nothing," she said quickly. "I told him that if he wanted to know, he ought to ask you."

His face relaxed. "Good girl. Margo is none of his business." His eyes warmed, softened. "Isn't she a beauty, Kenna? All fire and determination. A very strong woman with great business sense. I've never known anyone like her."

His voice had gone as soft as his eyes, and Kenna wanted to scream with jealousy. She couldn't remember ever hurting so much in her life. Oh, Denny, look at me, she pleaded silently. Look at me and love me for what I am, for what I could be....

But he only smiled that friendly charming smile that he always had ready. "How about making me a cup of coffee? And then we'll get the rest of the dictation out of the way. I might

let you go home early. I need a little extra time
by myself.''

Yes, because he was taking Margo to the
ballet and wanted to look his best, she thought
miserably. So she'd go home early, back to her
lonely apartment, and stare at the television
set. Because she didn't date. No one ever asked
her out, and she was far too shy to go to one of
the singles bars or invite men to her apartment.

''I'll get my pad and pen and be right
there,'' she said after a minute's hesitation,
and sighed as she followed him into his office.

When she got home she put on her jeans and
T-shirt and glared at herself in the mirror. The
jeans were too big and the shirt was too big
and she looked older than she was with her
hair hanging down around her face. Her eyes
weren't bad, though, and her mouth had a full,
nice shape. If only she could get rid of the rest
of her and just be eyes and a mouth, she might
catch Denny's eye. The thought amused her
and she grinned, turning away before the mirror could tell her how different she looked with
her face and eyes animated by laughter.

She turned on the television before she went
into the small kitchen to fix herself a sand-

wich for supper. She'd never had much appetite, but she seemed to have even less lately. Well, she wouldn't have to worry about getting fat, she told herself.

She walked around the dining room with her sandwich and cup of coffee in hand, smiling at the modest furniture. She enjoyed this apartment where she'd lived for the past two years. It wasn't expensive, but it was cozy and the green flowered sofa and matching chair looked friendly in the gray-carpeted room with its pale gray drapes. She'd splurged a month ago to redecorate the living room in a burst of early spring fever. Now it was really beginning to be spring, and she liked the new look. It made her feel brighter inside just looking at the furniture.

She watched television until bedtime, trying not to think about Denny out with Margo. She'd seen him in evening clothes before and remembered miserably how gorgeous he was in black. It emphasized his blond good looks. He was so handsome. A prince if there ever was one. Prince. That brought back Regan's horrible remark and she bristled again. Wasn't it bad enough that she had to listen to Denny moon over Margo without having to put up with Regan's evident dislike as well? She stormed off into the bedroom and went to bed before the memory had time to work her into a rage and keep her awake half the night thinking up horrible things to do to him.

The next morning she wore a beige sheath dress that clung lovingly to the curves of her slender body. The color did nothing for her, although the fit wasn't bad. She left her hair long, hating its frizzled look, but she didn't suppose it made that much difference. Denny never noticed the way she looked, anyway.

He was whistling when she got to the office, already pouring himself a cup of coffee and looking like a man on top of the world.

He turned when Kenna walked in and grinned. "There you are," he said. "Regan made coffee."

She flinched at the sound of his name and bit her tongue before she could say something foolish. "Did he?" she asked. "How nice."

"He's an early bird, all right."

She hung up her coat and uncovered the typewriter, then turned the appointment calendar to the right page and sat down.

"You're cheerful this morning," she said with a careful smile.

"I feel cheerful. I'm off to the lake Friday for a long weekend. Come to think of it, you might as well take Friday off, too, if Regan doesn't need you," he added.

For one wild, beautiful moment, she thought he might be going to ask her to go to the lake with him, and she beamed. The sudden radiance of her face captured his attention, and he frowned slightly.

"I'd like that," she told him.

"Got a date?" he asked.

"No," she said quickly, just in case.

"Too bad," he remarked, smiling dreamily as he stared at the other wall. "I'm taking Margo up to Lake Lanier with me for some fishing. Can you imagine, she likes to fish?"

Somewhere in Kenna's heart, a candle went out. "Oh, really?" she murmured calmly.

"I'm looking forward to the relaxation," he confessed. "I've been putting in twenty-four-hour days lately."

That was true, he did need the rest, but why did he have to take Margo, she wondered miserably.

"Well, we'd better get to it," he sighed. "The sooner we finish, the sooner we can leave. Grab your pad and come on . . ."

"Kenna!" came a muffled roar from Regan's office.

She gritted her teeth, casting a helpless glance in Denny's direction.

"Better go," he chuckled. "I'll wait my turn."

"Thanks, I'll do you a favor someday," she muttered, tossing him a dark look as she grabbed her pad and deliberately took her time going into Regan's office.

He knew she'd delayed on purpose, it was in his glittering dark eyes when she opened the door after a perfunctory knock and walked in. He was leaning back in his swivel chair, his jacket off, his broad chest rippling with muscles as he clasped his hands behind his head. Under the white shirt, she could see the thick shadow of dark hair, and the woman in her involuntarily appreciated the sheer masculinity of him.

"Yes, sir?" she asked sweetly.

He looked her up and down, and something in his eyes made her knees go weak. He was always appraising her, as if she were for sale, and it disturbed her more than she liked to admit. She tingled when those cold, dark eyes traced her body, feeling things she'd never ex-

perienced until he walked into her life. She
didn't know why she felt that way, and she
didn't like it. As a result, her hostility toward
him grew by leaps and bounds.

"The color stinks, but it's an improvement," he murmured.

She flushed, clenching the pad in her fingers. "You wanted something, Mr. Cole?"

He leaned forward. "I need to dictate a
couple of letters. Have a seat."

She started toward the chair, aware of his
eyes assessing her coldly.

"Have you been crying on my brother's
shoulder?" he asked suddenly.

She sat down heavily, gaping at him. "Sir?"

"You heard me. He asked me this morning
if I minded letting up on you."

Her chin came up. "I slay my own drag-
ons," she returned. "I don't need help."

He raised an eyebrow. "Should I be flattered? Yesterday I was a frog, today I'm a
dragon..."

"I didn't call you a frog, Mr. Cole," she reminded him.

"At any rate, that's the wrong fairy tale.
I've got something in mind for you, Cinderella," he murmured.

Her eyes widened, and he made an impatient sound. "Good God, I'm not that desperate for a woman," he growled, and she flushed angrily. "At any rate, this isn't the time to discuss it. Take a letter, Miss Dean . . ."

It only took fifteen minutes to finish the dictation, but she was almost shaking when she started out the door.

"Just a minute," Regan said behind her, his voice curt to the point of rudeness. "Denny's taking Friday off; did he mention it to you?"

She swallowed. "Yes, he did."

"Then presumably he told you why?" he added with narrowed eyes.

She only nodded.

"I'll be out of the office for a couple of days. But I'll expect you here Friday morning at 8:30 a.m. sharp. We're going to talk."

"About what?" she asked curtly.

"Well, Miss Dean," he said, leaning back again with his lips pursed, "you'll just have to wait and see, won't you? I'd like those letters as soon as they're typed. I have a case this morning."

"Yes, sir," she said, and forced herself to walk out without asking any more questions.

Denny was sympathetic when she told him that Regan wouldn't let her off.

"I guess it's that criminal case he's handling," he sighed. "Well, that's the breaks," he added with a sheepish grin. "We tried."

"We tried," she agreed, and her eyes clung lovingly to his handsome face. It was so pleasant to sit and look at him, to be with him. Oh, if only she were beautiful like Margo.

"By the way," he said, "would you call the florist and have them send Margo a dozen red roses?"

She jotted it down, keeping her eyes lowered so he wouldn't see the sudden pain in them. "Red, hmmm?" she teased, putting up a brave front.

"Red, for love," he laughed. "She's a tiger, my Margo. Spicy and passionate, every man's dream."

"Do I hear wedding bells in the distance?" she murmured, and stiffened as she waited for the answer.

He sighed, toying with a pencil on the desk blotter. "That would depend on the lady," he murmured. "She's not much for cages. But speaking for myself, I'm more than ready to put a ring on her finger. I've never known anyone like her.''

She wanted to scream and throw things. Instead, she smiled and reminded him about a letter they needed to get out on a case that they'd just won. He grinned and started dictating. And if his secretary's face was strained and paler than usual, he didn't notice.

Chapter Two

She wore the frontier outfit deliberately Friday morning just to irritate Regan, because she knew he didn't like it. If he thought he was going to dominate her like he dominated everything and everybody else around him, he had another think coming.

She hung up her light coat and uncovered her typewriter, grumbling steadily. Since Denny was out of the office—she didn't want to think about where—she'd only have to get the mail for Regan. But he'd want it yesterday, so she headed for the door and in her haste almost collided with Regan, who was coming through it.

He lifted a bushy eyebrow at the quick rush of color that tinted her high cheekbones.

"Do you do it deliberately?" he asked her, unblinking, unsmiling, blocking her path with his cowhide attaché case.

"Do what . . . deliberately?" she asked.

"Make yourself as unattractive as possible."

It was the first time she'd ever raised her hand to a man in her life. But she took a swing at him with all her frustration and wounded pride behind it.

He caught her wrist before she connected, jerking her back into the office and booting the door closed with his foot. Without breaking stride, ignoring her faint struggles, he half-dragged her into his own office and slammed the door behind them.

She felt the clasp of his fingers with a sense of wonder at the new, unfamiliar sensations his touch was causing. She'd never tingled like that. Perhaps it was temper, but then why was her breathing so shallow? She disliked the surge of emotion, and her eyes narrowed angrily as she glared up at him.

He dropped the attaché case on the floor and caught her other wrist as well, just holding her there in front of him until she stopped struggling and stood still, panting with smothered rage.

When he saw that she was through swinging, he dropped her wrists and glared down his formidable nose at her.

"If you ever lift your hand to me again, it'll be the last time," he warned in his courtroom voice, deep and cold.

Her lower lip trembled briefly with the suppressed hatred that filled her stiff body. "If you ever insult me like that again, it'll be the last time, too, counselor," she tossed back, her voice choked with emotion. "I'll walk out the door, and you can find some stacked blonde with knee-deep cleavage to replace me, and see if she can type your contracts and your briefs and your petitions in between polishing her nails!"

"Calm down, Kenna," he said after a minute. "Sit down, honey."

He pushed her gently down into a big, leather armchair and perched himself on the edge of the huge polished wood desk. He gave her time to gather herself together, lighting a cigarette and taking a deep draw before he spoke.

"Don't call me *honey*," she bit off.

"Denny does. So do half the attorneys who walk in that door. Why not me?"

"Because . . ." She stared up at him, her lips parting as she tried to picture Regan ever saying the word and meaning it, with his dark eyes blazing with passion. Her own thoughts embarrassed her and she caught a deep breath, looking at his black leather shoes instead. "Oh, never mind."

"He's getting involved with Margo," he said quietly. "And I don't just mean involved in bed. It looks as if he's thinking about marriage, and I don't want him married to her."

She felt sick all over again as he confirmed what Denny had already admitted. Denny, married! The thought was more than she could bear.

"Stop looking like the heroine of a Victorian melodrama, for God's sake." He spoke so sharply that she sat straight up. "He isn't married yet!"

"How are you going to stop him?" she asked miserably.

"I'm not. You are."

She blinked. "Excuse me, I'm always dim before I've had my morning coffee and my supply of razor blades."

His mouth tugged up, a rare show of amusement that made her feel strange when she saw it. "You're going to save him from Margo."

She cocked her head and studied him blatantly. "You don't look like the fairy godmother to me, Mr. Internationally Famous Trial Lawyer. And I don't have a pumpkin to my name. And if you'll take a good, long look at me several things will immediately occur to you. The first is that I'm drab," she admitted painfully, "the second is that I have no looks to speak of, and the third is that I've been here almost two years and the most intimate thing your brother has ever said to me is, 'Kenna, how about a cup of coffee?'"

He didn't laugh. He took another draw from the cigarette, and his eyes were busy, bold, and slow as they took her apart from the face down.

"Taking inventory?" she muttered.

"In a manner of speaking." His eyes fell on the too-ruffled blouse. "Do you wear a bra?"

She caught her breath at the sheer impudence of the question.

"And do, please, try not to faint while you're thinking up an answer, Cinders," he said with a mocking smile. "I'm trying to find out if you're naturally flat-chested, or if you simply overlook the fact that breasts need support to be noticed."

Her face was bloodred and she stood up. "Mr. Cole . . ."

"My housekeeper calls me that." He caught her shoulder and jerked her against him, bending her arm back so that she was helpless. "Tell me, or I'll find out for myself," he threatened, and his free hand came up to hover over her blouse.

"Oh, for God's sake!" she squeaked. "All right, I don't wear one!"

He let her go, watching with amusement as she hid behind the chair and then gaped at him over it.

"Are you crazy?" she burst out.

"No, but you sure as hell are repressed," he replied. "Twenty-five, isn't it?"

"We aren't all wildly permissive," she said, choking.

"I begin to get the picture," he nodded. "Not much of a social life, I'll bet."

"I date!" she threw back.

He blinked. "Date what? You don't look as if you've ever been kissed . . . or did you think that would get you pregnant?" he asked with an outrageous smile.

She glanced at the trash can, measuring it for his head. He followed her gaze and chuckled softly.

"Go ahead, honey," he dared her in a soft voice. "Try it."

"I wish I were a man; I'd cream you!" she burst out.

"Haven't you ever heard of women's lib?" he asked casually. "Men aren't supposed to be superior anymore. Come on, honey, throw a punch at me."

"Do I look stupid?" she asked, taking in the sheer size of the man. "On second thought, if I were a man, I wouldn't come at you with anything less than a bazooka!"

"That might be wise," he agreed. He leaned back against the desk, unusually attractive in his navy blue pin-striped suit. She always noticed his clothes; he had a flair for picking styles and colors that gave him a towering elegance.

"Anyway," he continued, bending to crush out his cigarette, an action that strained the material across his muscular arms and his broad back, "what I have in mind is transforming you."

She stared at him warily. "I'm not sure I want to be transformed."

"Don't be ridiculous, of course you do." He glanced up and down at what he could see of her figure behind the tall chair. "First order of business is going to be a haircut. I know long hair is supposed to be sexy, but yours looks like barbed wire most of the time."

"Oh, you're just great for my ego," she ground out.

"And the second order of business is a bra," he continued, unabashed, his eyes narrowing. "Don't you know that the worst thing you can do is sag?"

"There's not enough of me to sag," she said miserably, avoiding his eyes.

"I'd bet there is," he returned, not unkindly. "You're tall, and you have nice legs. You have a natural elegance of carriage that could work well for you. And with the right makeup, the right clothes..." He pursed his lips, nodding. "I think you might be more than enough to catch my brother's wandering eye."

"You've forgotten something," she advised.

He cocked a bushy eyebrow. "What? Your teeth are all right," he began.

"Oh, thanks, and they're all my own too!"

He chuckled softly. "You'll do. Well? Do you want to be alone for the rest of your life, or do you want to take a chance?"

"I can't," she said, exasperated, as she came reluctantly around the chair. "What you're talking about costs money, and I'm not independently wealthy. All I have is my salary, and out of it has to come my rent, utilities, groceries, clothes..."

"I'll take care of it," he told her.

"Like fun you will," she tossed back, her eyes flaring up.

"I said I'll take care of it," he replied. "It was my idea, and it's my brother I'm trying to save from that Latin temptress. I don't want a money-hungry tramp in my family."

"No, you'd rather have a secretary with no money, no connections, no social position..."

"Do I look like a snob?" he asked incredulously.

"I didn't mean it like that," she confessed. She drew in a deep, steadying breath. "Anyway, what's Denny going to think if he knows you're footing the bill?"

"He won't know," he promised, "because we're not going to tell him. I'll pick you up Saturday morning at your apartment, and we'll get started. Make yourself an appointment with Frederickson's downtown."

"But they're horribly expensive!" she protested.

"Make the appointment early," he continued, "because when we finish there, we're going to Almon's to have you outfitted."

Almon's was a charming boutique with a resident designer and some of the trendiest new styles in the country. She stared at him as if she couldn't believe her eyes.

"You'll go to the ball, Cinderella," he promised. "Even if you have to ride in a Mercedes instead of a coach drawn by white horses."

"There isn't a ball..."

"There most certainly is, next Saturday night at the Biltmore, and I'm taking you." He shot back his white cuff and looked at his watch. "And that's all the time we have this morning. Get back to your ashes, and don't breathe a word to Denny next week. I'm going to have a photographer along just to capture his expression when he sees the new you."

"Could he get my expression while he's at it?" she asked hopefully. "I'll need something to convince me I'm not dreaming."

He looked at her for a long, long time before he spoke, unsmiling. "Have you ever had an expensive gown?"

She avoided his eyes and walked toward the door. "The only way I'm going to have one now is if I get to pay you back, counselor. I mean that," she added, looking over her shoulder. "I pay my own way, frugal though it may be."

"All right, we'll deduct a little from your check each week," he agreed, moving around behind his desk. "When you make the coffee, how about bringing me a cup?"

She nodded and closed the door quietly behind her. She went down to get the mail in a daze and wondered if her unfulfilled longing for Denny had finally pushed her over the brink into insanity. The morning had been unreal.

Chapter Three

Kenna hadn't given Regan directions to her apartment, but he seemed to know the way. She had just finished dressing in slacks and a long-sleeved blouse and sweater when the doorbell rang at eight-thirty sharp the next morning.

Regan spared her a brief glance from hooded eyes. "Ready?" he asked carelessly, looking as if he were regretting the whole thing already. "Let's go, I'm double parked."

She followed him into the elevator, approving of his casual slacks, deep burgundy-colored velour shirt, and tweed jacket. The shirt was open at the throat, and she saw a glimpse of darkly tanned skin and thick, very thick hair in the opening. It made him look even more masculine, more threatening, and she wished she'd never agreed to this. Being around him at the office was bad enough, but this was... unnerving.

"I won't rape you, I promise," he said out of the blue, cocking an eyebrow at her as she retreated to the other side of the elevator.

"If you did, you'd be disappointed," she sighed, not rising to the bait. "Twenty-five-year-old virgins aren't much in demand these days."

He seemed shocked at the comeback, and she grinned at him.

"I'm not a Victorian miss, as you reminded me the other day," she said with a sheepish grin. "but you knocked me off balance. I had you pictured as a very staid type who wouldn't even suggest anything remotely sexual around a woman."

"My God, were you off base," he remarked.

"So were you." She sighed. "I may not be a stacked blonde, and I may look like a frump, but I don't faint at the thought of a man's bedroom. It's just that I've never wanted to occupy one." She glared at him. "And the reason I don't wear a bra is because it's the mark of a liberated woman!''

The elevator door had just opened, and a little old lady with blue-tinted hair actually gasped as she heard that last impassioned statement.

Kenna stared at the elderly woman and slowly went beet-red. ''Oh, my gosh,'' she groaned.

Regan, trying to keep a straight face, caught Kenna by the arm and half-dragged her out of the elevator and through the lobby.

''Liberated woman,'' he scoffed, giving her a mocking glance. ''You might as well give up the act; I know pure bravado when I see it.''

She sighed. ''I can't even act like a normal woman,'' she grumbled, jamming her hands in her pockets. ''No wonder Denny doesn't notice me.''

''I notice you.''

She didn't even look up. ''When you want a cup of coffee or a letter typed, you do.''

He stopped and turned to face her, and she looked up to find his dark, steady eyes holding her own.

''I know what it is to be lonely, Kenna,'' he said quietly. ''I know how it feels to look around and wonder if the world would ever miss you if you died.''

"You've got all kinds of women,'' she faltered.

"I've got money. Of course I can have women,'' he said with a cynical smile. "I've even been married, did you know?''

That was faintly shocking. Denny never talked about Regan's private life. "No,'' she admitted.

"Jessica was twenty-six. Blond and blue-eyed and as perfect as a dream. The marriage lasted exactly a year.''

She saw a flash of raw emotion in his face. "Were you divorced?'' she asked.

"No,'' he replied curtly. "She died.''

"Oh. I'm sorry,'' she said gently, and meant it.

His hands idly moved up and down on her arms. "It's been almost three years. I'm older and wiser. But there are nights when...'' He let go of her and moved away to light a cigarette, and she realized for the first time that he was, indeed, a lonely man. It was a shock to realize that she cared that he was lonely.

"Life is too short to try living it in the past,'' he remarked after a minute. He turned. "And far too short to long for things and not try to go and get them. Isn't Denny worth a few changes in your life?''

She had always thought so. ''Yes,'' she said, giving herself a mental shake. ''Of course he is.''

''Then let's see what we can do to get his attention.''

The first stop was the beauty salon. She watched her long, dark hair fall in strands onto the spotless floor while Mr. Andrew snipped and discussed the latest styles and called back and forth to other patrons. Kenna found herself caught up in the cheerful surroundings and the excitement of doing herself over. Perhaps Regan was right. She was twenty-five, and it was time she took herself in hand. It was time she started to live.

When her hair was washed and blow-dried, she stared blankly at the girl in the mirror. She'd forgone makeup that morning, and now she was glad. With her rosy cheeks and full, soft mouth and unadorned eyes, she looked fresh and natural. And the short, beautifully-shaped hair framed her face in darkness, making her look like a pixie with her slightly slanted eyes, thin brows, and high cheek-bones. She grinned at herself wonderingly.

"Is nice, no?" Mr. Andrew chuckled. "Now, miss, you go to makeup counter and have face done and see difference. I promise, you like."

She did that, finding herself with an extra half hour before she was to meet Regan in the couture department. She watched, fascinated, as the makeup expert did her face like a canvas, outlining her lips in plum and filling them with a deep, rich magenta, then delicately tinting her cheeks and eyebrows, lengthening her lashes, shadowing her eyes and finally enhancing her lovely complexion with the faintest touch of powder.

"Is that me?" she asked after a minute, captivated by the difference, wondering at the girl with the small, straight nose and big, shimmering green eyes and soft oval of a face with its bee-stung mouth.

"Quite a difference," the makeup expert agreed with a smile. She sold Kenna the right cosmetics to keep the new look daily and waved her off.

Regan was wandering around the mannequins with a dark scowl, sizing up each dress, while the saleslady darted curious glances his way.

"Waiting for me?" Kenna asked from behind him.

He turned, still scowling, and his eyes widened suddenly as he recognized her. "My God." It was all he said, but the inflection was enough to convey his meaning. He walked around her, staring. "Well, well, Cinderella, you do have something."

"While you're trying to figure out what," she said, "couldn't we go into the budget shop and look for clothes? I'm going to owe you my soul if we have to buy anything in here. They don't even have price tags on most of these things!"

"You're going to a ball, not a beach party," he said curtly. "I'm not taking you to the Biltmore in a dress off the rack."

"But..."

"Oh, shut up," he said impatiently, and taking her arm, he led her to the saleslady. While she stood rigidly, Regan told the tall, thin elderly woman exactly what he wanted for Kenna and then waited impatiently while the saleslady went off to search through her stock.

She came back in a minute with a long, sensuous confection of green-, gold-, and aqua-patterned Quiana with a low criss-cross neckline.

"This is one of our designer models," the woman said with a smile. "And perfect for a figure like yours, my dear," she added to Kenna.

"Well, try it on," Regan said. "Then come out here and let me see it."

The saleslady sent Kenna into the back, where she tried on the dress in front of the long mirror in the plush dressing room. She stared at herself as if entranced.

"How does it fit, my dear... oh, my," the saleslady murmured approvingly as Kenna walked out of the fitting room.

"It fits like a dream," she said sheepishly, almost afraid to touch the silky material for fear of running it. "Like gossamer..."

"The color is perfect," the older woman agreed. "Just perfect, with that light tan of yours."

She led Kenna back out into the showroom and stood with hands folded, while her client moved forward toward the tall dark man who was waiting for her. Regan was idly watching passersby when he heard Kenna's step and turned.

He didn't say anything. His eyes went up and down and up again, and his face hardened.

"Is—is it all right?" she asked, desperately wanting to be told that she looked stunning, that Denny would fall at her feet . . . anything.

He nodded. "Yes," he said in a strange, husky tone, "it's all right. Now see what you can find for the office. A tailored suit, some skirts and blouses that don't look frumpy, and a couple of ensembles for leisure."

"But . . . but what for?" she asked.

"Going out with me one time isn't going to give Denny any hints," he said curtly. "Or did you expect him to take one look at you and drop to his knees to propose?"

She hated that cynical question. The dress had made her feel like a princess, and now he had spoiled it all. "No," she admitted. "I didn't expect that." She turned, but he caught her bare arm and held her back, out of earshot of the saleslady.

"You look enchanting, is that what you want to hear?" he asked at her ear, his voice husky, his breath warm against her neck.

"That dress makes a man want to smooth it away from your body and see what's underneath."

She caught her breath at the blatant seduction of his voice.

"Embarrassed?" he chuckled as he let her go. "Well, you wanted to know, didn't you?"

She rushed off before he could manage anything worse and was surprised at the furious beat of her heart when she went to take off the dress.

It was the most wonderful shopping trip she'd ever been on. She bought a two-piece suit, pink with a plum feather pattern; it had a straight skirt and a long-sleeved V-neck jacket secured by a plum-colored rose at the peplum waist. She bought several skirts and revealing blouses that she wouldn't have looked at if Regan hadn't been with her, forcing her to buy them despite her own misgivings. She bought an expensive bra that added at least one size to her small breasts and some lacy lingerie. And as she mentally calculated the cost on the way out of the store, she sighed.

"I'll be working for you for the rest of my life," she murmured.

He glanced down at her from his superior height and smiled. "Would you mind? As long as I made the coffee once in a while?"

The tone of his deep voice surprised her into looking up. And when she did, she felt a warm surge of sensation that rippled down to her feet. His eyes, dark and quiet and intense, held hers until the jostling of passersby broke their strange exchanged look and brought them back to reality.

"Thank you for going with me," she murmured, following him out to his gray Porsche.

"I didn't have a choice," he said, glancing sharply at her as he unlocked the door and helped her inside. "Left on your own, you'd have come back with the same clothes you thought looked great on you before." He went around the car and eased his formidable bulk in beside her. She glared for all she was worth.

"I am not stupid about clothes," she informed him.

"Your idea of fashion is a gunny sack with arm and neck holes," he replied as he started the sleek car.

"Well, it's better than looking like a prostitute," she tossed back, "and that's what I'll look like in some of those things you made me buy! The neckline on one of those blouses is halfway to my knees!''

"Don't exaggerate," he said shortly. His dark eyes dropped to her T-shirt. "How many of those damned things do you have, anyway?"

"What things?" she demanded.

"Those shapeless things you hide your body in."

"I like loose clothing," she retorted.

"Obviously." He threw a careless arm over the back of the seat as he turned to back the car out of the parking space. His face was much too close to hers. Involuntarily, her eyes went to his wide, chiseled mouth, and she wondered what it would feel like to kiss him.

He stopped the car to put it in gear, but he didn't move. She sensed the sudden heavy beat of his heart, the warmth of his body.

"Look at me," he growled.

She looked up and her eyes were held by his, possessed by his, so that the world was suddenly contained in a pair of intense brown eyes under thick, short lashes.

His gaze dropped to her soft, parted lips, and he moved fractionally, his own lips parting. She waited, and wanted, hardly breathing, and her eyes narrowed to slits as he came closer. She drank in the scent of his cologne, the warmth of his big body, the faintly smoky scent of his breath as she felt it against her lips. And she wanted to kiss him with a longing that had her spinning. She wanted to kiss him hungrily and hard and see if the touch of that chiseled mouth would be as maddening as she was imagining it would . . .

"Get going, will you!" The loud voice was followed by the equally loud blaring of a car horn.

The dark brown eyes blinked and Regan looked into the rear-view mirror with vague curiosity, while Kenna felt herself trembling with hunger for a kiss she wouldn't get. She wanted to jump out of the car and kick the driver behind them for interrupting. Why she should feel that way when she loved Denny was something she didn't dare question. She cleared her throat.

Abruptly Regan put the car into forward and eased down on the accelerator, glancing toward her as he left the irate driver behind them. "Would you mind telling me what that long, soulful look was all about?" he asked, a bite in his deep voice.

She swallowed. "I wasn't looking at you. I was thinking," she countered weakly.

"About what?" he asked as he pulled into traffic.

"You mentioned that taking me out one time wouldn't be enough," she murmured, nervous with him all of a sudden. "What did you mean? You said we were just going to transform me..."

"It's going to take more than a haircut and new clothes to do that," he said flatly. He lit a cigarette while they stopped at a red light. "And going out with me is the best way I know to catch Denny's attention. Or haven't you noticed how competitive he is with me?"

"I don't know if my ego can take more than one date with you," she said matter-of-factly, glaring at him.

"It will have to, if you really want Denny," he told her. "And I'm not going to pull my punches. I'm going to teach you how to dress, how to walk, how to flirt, the works. Because what you need most is confidence, and you're sadly lacking in that commodity."

"And you think having my appearance torn to pieces is going to give it to me," she mused ironically.

"Ultimately," he agreed. His eyes scanned her briefly. "I'd bet good money that you spent every high-school dance standing with your back to the wall, slouched, your arms folded across what bosom you've got, praying for some boy to ask you to dance."

She gasped and blushed all at once, because he was dead right. She couldn't even manage to look at him, and involuntarily her arms folded defensively across her breasts.

"How did you manage to get so repressed?" he asked. "Didn't your mother spend any time showing you all those little tricks women use to hook men?"

"I didn't have a mother," she replied. "She and Dad were divorced when I was young. I lived with him and my stepmother until I grew up and went out on my own. My stepmother let me stay on sufferance, but we avoided each other whenever possible. Does that answer your question?"

Her tone would have cut a lesser man dead, but Regan only lifted an eyebrow. "Have you seen your mother since?"

She shook her head. "She died a few years ago. Look, can we talk about something else?"

He took a long draw from the cigarette. "Have you ever been serious about a man?"

She laughed shortly, bitterly. "I've never had the chance," she confessed coldly. "Men these days are only interested in sex. If you say no on the first date, they don't come back."

"And that's a lot of bull," he shot back. "You aren't going to convince me that every man you dated tried to rape you the minute you climbed in a car with him."

Startled, she glanced at him. "I didn't mean it that way," she said. "I only meant . . ." She drew in a slow breath. "Oh, what's the use? I've only been out with four men in my life, and two of them were blind dates. And of course they didn't try to rape me, they couldn't get me home fast enough."

"Did it hurt to admit that to me?"

"Yes, if you want to know," she said curtly. She fumbled in her pocketbook and fished out her glasses, unfolding them to perch them on her nose. "And I'm tired of seeing blurs instead of people, I'm half blind without these."

He laughed softly. "Then why weren't you wearing them this morning?"

"I figured that if I could see how I looked in those things you made me buy, I wouldn't buy them," she grumbled.

"Ostrich," he accused.

"That's me. You were right about the dances, you know," she added miserably. "I've always slouched because I hate being so tall. And now I'll slouch because of those incredible necklines."

"No, you won't. Not when I get through with you."

"I'm not at all sure I want to be what you're going to make me into," she murmured. "Denny may not like me that way."

"He likes Margo that way," he said with cruel emphasis and a cold smile. "And I hope you're not naive enough to think they're up at Lake Lanier playing checkers?"

She flushed to the roots of her dark hair. "Margo has a lot going for her."

"So I hear," he replied flatly. "But I'd guess it's not so much what she's got as what she does with it, honey. Like all attractive women, she probably makes the most of her assets."

"How is it that you know so much about fashion and flair?" she asked curtly, glancing toward him.

He stared straight ahead with eyes that were momentarily blank. "Jessica was a top fashion model," he said, his voice quiet and soft in memory.

"Oh." She looked away from him, embarrassed by the emotion in his deep voice.

He crushed out the cigarette with faint violence. "Denny will notice you before we're through, I promise you that."

"I know why I don't like Margo, but why don't you? You haven't even met her," she noted when he was pulling up in front of her apartment.

He cut off the engine and leaned back against his door, studying her. "Because I sense that she's more woman than Denny's going to be able to handle. She'll have him standing in the corner like a coatrack before she's through. Besides that," he added darkly, "I don't know beans about her background, and that bothers me. Denny could be getting into something over his head."

"You mean, she could be a secret agent or something?"

"My, what wide eyes," he murmured. "I mean, Denny is wealthy and stands to be a lot wealthier. From what he's told me, she's the type of lady who wants to be well-kept. It isn't hard for a woman to want a rich man, Kenna,'' he said with bitter humor. ''Denny deserves more than that.''

She stared down at her folded hands. Yes, he did. She herself loved him, after all. She could give him love, if nothing else.

''I'll pick you up at two tomorrow afternoon,'' he said. ''And we'll start the lessons. You can wear one of your new outfits.''

She lifted her head and blinked, staring at him. ''Tomorrow?''

''I assume you don't have a heavy date lined up?''

She glowered. ''Wouldn't it shock you if I did?''

''The way you dress,'' he said derisively, ''it would.''

''If you have your way, I'll be walking the streets naked,'' she burst out.

''That,'' he returned shortly, ''would be worse than what you're wearing.''

She could have thrown her purse at him. She couldn't remember ever in her life feeling this kind of maniacal rage toward a man—the same rage that had made her fling that file folder at his proud head. But it seemed to get worse every time she was with him.

He was already out of the car with the shopping bags before she could find her voice, and she led him stoically up to her small apartment.

"How did you find my apartment building?" she asked, as he opened the door and let her go in first.

"I asked Denny where you lived. He looked it up." He glanced at her as he dumped the packages on her colorful sofa. "Obviously, he's never been here."

She shook her head sadly, and then she laughed. "Nobody's been here, except family and an occasional girl friend."

He jammed his hands in his pockets and looked around him. "Too bad you don't dress like you decorate," he said finally. "The room has personality."

"And I haven't?" she murmured defensively, bristling again.

"I don't know," he replied. His dark eyes went over her withdrawn face. "I've never paid much attention to you."

"That's not surprising," she sighed. "I've seen photographs of the women you go around with."

His eyebrows went straight up. "Meaning?"

She laughed self-consciously. "Some of them make even Margo look ugly by comparison."

He pulled out a cigarette and lit it, studying her curiously. "I get lonely. Don't you?"

Her eyes widened with something like shock. She was beginning to realize that he was human after all, not the ogre of her imagination. Perhaps he missed his late wife. It didn't make her like him any better, but it helped her to understand him better.

"Everyone gets lonely, I expect," she hedged, turning away. Some more than others, she added silently, like me, wanting a man I can't have.

"And that's your whole problem, Kenna," he growled. "You walk around hunched over with your head hanging, feeling sorry for yourself. My God, no wonder you're twenty-five and living alone!"

She whirled gracefully, like a ballerina, her eyes reckless with challenge. Anger made her whole face come alive.

"I like living alone!" she tossed back.

"Like hell you do," he countered. "How much television can you watch before you get sick of it and your own company?"

She felt her lower lip trembling with indignation. He was hitting too close to home. "Don't you have someplace to go?" she asked coldly.

"As a matter of fact, I have a date tonight," he said cruelly, smiling at her involuntary grimace. "I won't be sitting home alone hoping for the phone to ring."

Her eyes clouded with mingled fury and hurt. "She must have been desperate, to go out with you!" she flung at him, even though she was positive it was the other way around.

He only smiled with quiet confidence. He had the look of a man who knew everything there was to know about women, and his gaze was so frankly sensual that she was shocked. She hadn't realized before just how sexy he was. She didn't want to think about it now, either; it disturbed her.

She turned away. "I have things to do."

"So have I. I'll pick you up at two tomorrow." He opened the door and went out without a backward glance, leaving her to fume silently and alone.

Chapter Four

Kenna spent a sleepless night, full of dreams in which she took Denny away from Margo and he carried her off to a castle to live happily ever after. But she woke up to a lonely apartment and a day she dreaded. It was hard enough putting up with Regan Cole at the office. How in the world was she going to stand hours of forced companionship with the man without murdering him?

She got dressed an hour before he came to pick her up, defiantly choosing a pair of designer jeans and a white turtleneck. That ought to burn him up, she thought, grinning at her reflection in the mirror. She'd done her face as the cosmetics expert had taught her, and the difference, even with her glasses on, was something to write home about. She couldn't wait for Denny to see her tomorrow.

The doorbell rang at two-thirty sharp, and she opened the door reluctantly.

Regan, dressed in tan slacks and an open-throated black and tan shirt, glared at her. "Why didn't you just wear the sack you brought that home in?" he demanded.

She glared up at him. It was a long way, because this afternoon she was wearing ballerina shoes with flat heels. She'd never been more conscious of the sheer size of him.

"I'm only spending the afternoon with *you*," she tossed back. "I didn't see any reason to try looking seductive."

His eyebrows arched. "I thought the whole idea of this exercise was to teach you to be exactly that—seductive. Not," he added coldly, "for my benefit, you needn't worry about that. We've already agreed that you're not my type."

"Thank goodness," she sighed with a sarcastic smile. She turned. "In that case, I'll put on one of those slit-to-the-navel numbers you made me buy."

"Don't wear longjohns under it," he called after her. "And put on a bra!"

She slammed her bedroom door as hard as she could.

Ten minutes later, she slunk back into the living room, feeling self-conscious and about as seductive as a hunk of cheese.

He turned from a brooding contemplation of the photos she kept on her coffee table and stared at her. The new blouse was a pale olive. It had cap sleeves and a neckline that ended just between her breasts, hinting at their soft curves. The bra she'd bought to wear with it gave her the appearance of grander assets than she possessed, and the color of the blouse brought out the deep green of her eyes.

"Stand up straight, for God's sake," he growled, rising from the couch.

She did, but her eyes told him what she thought of the comment.

"You walk like a mortician," he remarked, leading the way to the door.

"At least I don't look like one," she said, staring pointedly at his grim face.

"That's debatable," he said imperturbably. "Let's go."

"Why can't we stay here?" she asked curtly.

"Afraid to be alone in your apartment with me?" he asked with a malicious smile.

"I'm hardly in a position to worry about my honor," she reminded him sweetly as they walked to the elevator, "if I have to be taught how to seduce a man." She glared up at him as the elevator stopped and the door began to slide open. "Aren't we lucky that I don't have to lure *you* into my bed?"

The same elderly lady who'd listened to her opinions on bras the day before stood stock-still in the elevator, staring at the red-faced girl and the tall man. She seemed to be debating whether or not to get out.

"My, my, what a lovely day...isn't it?" The sweet little lady faltered and muttered an apology as she rushed out of the elevator and down the hall.

Regan was trying to keep a straight face as he held the elevator door for Kenna. He pushed the ground floor button and glanced at her.

"Does she lie in wait for you?" he asked.

She sighed. "Up until this weekend, she thought I was a nice, retiring young lady with admirable moral principles."

"Do you mind what people think?" he asked suddenly.

She glanced up at him, wondering at the sudden shock that went through her when she met his unblinking gaze. She looked away quickly, oddly disturbed. "No, I don't think so," she replied.

"Then why lock yourself in that apartment like a hermit and deliberately dress yourself into the woodwork?" he asked.

She stared at the floor of the elevator. "Because I don't drink or do drugs," she said quietly. "I don't believe in free sex, and I'd rather be walking in the woods than dancing to a disco beat."

He didn't say a word, but his eyes didn't move away from her bent head until the elevator stopped.

"Come on, diamond girl," he murmured, letting her precede him out of the elevator.

"What?" she asked, surprised into looking up.

"Diamond in the rough," he murmured. "All you need is a little polishing."

"That could be painful," she said, trying to make light of it.

"Cinderella didn't get the prince without a little suffering, honey," he reminded her.

She sighed. "I feel more like the pumpkin than Cinderella right now, thanks."

"That's what we're going to work on."

She followed him out to his car, apprehensive and not a little nervous. Regan bothered her; being with him made her feel shaky. If only she'd never agreed to this! But if there was a chance in a million that he could make her noticeable to Denny, she'd take it, and gladly. No sacrifice was too great to catch Denny's eye, not even spending time with a man she disliked intensely.

Regan lived in a luxurious apartment in downtown Atlanta, overlooking the Regency Hyatt House's distinctive saucer and the night lights that made Atlanta look like a many-colored jewel. The whole apartment was carpeted in thick gray pile and decorated with Mediterranean furniture and bold gray-and-beige-striped curtains at the windows. There were a lot of carved wooden sculptures and animals that had a distinctively African flavor, including the masks on the wall. An antique table held a single photograph in a small, ornate frame. She knew without being told who it was, that beautiful blonde with the long, windblown hair. It was Jessica.

"Don't stand on ceremony," he growled from behind her. "You might as well ask me about it."

She flushed, embarrassed at being caught in her scrutiny. She turned, looking up with apologetic eyes. "I'm sorry," she said quietly. "She was very lovely."

His eyes clouded and he turned away, his hands jammed deep in his pockets. "Sit down."

She moved toward the sofa and sank into it ungracefully.

"That's where we start," he said, surveying her narrowly. "You don't even sit like a woman, you attack chairs as if you were afraid they might leap up and bite."

She clamped her teeth together. It was going to be a long session, and she could see that holding her temper was going to cause her some problems.

But somehow she managed to make it through the long afternoon, while she was told everything that she did wrong and how to correct it, right down to picking up cups and holding them gracefully in her hand.

"I can't imagine how I lived to be this old all by myself," she said sweetly when he called it a day.

"Neither can I," he agreed infuriatingly. "One more thing, think feline. Be conscious of your body as an expression of grace in movement. Walk seductively."

"Maybe you could take me down on the streets, and I could watch the experts ... ?"

He glowered at her. "There's a difference between seductiveness and blatant sexuality. Haven't you ever noticed models move down the runway in fashion shows?"

"I never really paid that much attention," she confessed.

"There are fashion shows telecast over the cable network," he told her. "Start watching them. It wouldn't hurt to enroll in a ballet class."

"That's where I draw the line," she told him shortly. "I don't have time to prance around with preteens in a tutu."

His eyes went down her body slowly, appraisingly. "Let's see you walk, Cinderella," he said.

She took a deep breath and tried to remember everything he'd drummed into her reeling mind. She moved with conscious grace, her body gently swaying like a windblown reed, her face held high, her steps easy, and the lines of her body straight and tall.

His dark eyes flashed and narrowed as she approached him. His gaze dropped pointedly to the thrust of her small breasts.

She flushed at the intimacy of the look, and her jaw tightened.

"Not bad," he murmured curtly. "For a rank beginner," he added, lifting his eyes to hers. "But you've got a hell of a long way to go, and not a lot of time. Margo's got the jump on you, honey."

"I know that," she muttered miserably. "And the body to go with it."

"There isn't a damned thing wrong with yours," he said, his eyes leaving her in no doubt that he meant it. "All you need to do is to learn how to use it."

She felt her toes tingle. "If you mean what I think you do, you can just forget it! I don't have any intention of trying to get Denny into my bed!"

His mouth curled up at one corner. "Don't you want him?"

"Of course I do, but not...well, not like that...I mean," she faltered, avoiding his probing stare. What did she mean? She loved Denny, of course she wanted him...she guessed. How could she know, though? He'd never tried to touch her that way in all the two years she'd known him.

"Do you know what you mean?" he asked. He moved closer, and the sheer size of him was intimidating. He smelled of spice and tobacco, and he was warm....

"Look at me. Flirt with your eyes," he murmured, watching her. "Let's see what you've learned."

She managed to meet his dark gaze. She smiled shyly and dropped her own, to raise them again and let them glance off his, and treat him to a gentle flutter of her long lashes.

"Better?" she murmured, raising her face.

His eyes were unusually dark and he didn't answer for a minute. "You've got possibilities," he said finally. "Are your lashes real?"

"Of course," she said. She blinked, surprised at the question. Then she noticed his own lashes, thick and dark, making a perfect frame for his very dark eyes. They were nearly black, and his complexion was olive, darker than she'd realized before.

His eyes caught hers and held them, and a long, searching exchange built the tension until she felt her knees tremble at the intensity of it. It was like touching a live wire, and she had to tear her eyes from his.

Her lips parted on a nervous breath. She moved away from him, away from the sudden magnetism of his big body. "I guess I'd better get home," she said in a voice that sounded oddly strange.

"I guess you had," he agreed. "By the way, I've arranged for Denny to be out of town all next week. The first time he'll see your new look will be Saturday night at the ball."

"Where is he?" she asked, suddenly miserable. She'd looked forward to Denny seeing her tomorrow and now he wouldn't be there.

"Don't look so tragic," he chided. He lit a cigarette and turned. "He's in New York, doing some leg work for me. Or so he believes. He grumbled too. Margo's still here," he added with a wicked smile.

Her heart leaped. "Putting some breathing space between them, huh, fairy godfather?" she murmured with a grin.

He turned, catching the amused light in her eyes. He stopped, just looking at her until she flushed and lowered her gaze to his broad chest. That was even worse. She could see the thick mat of hair that obviously covered his muscular body, and it had a strange effect on her.

"That was the idea, all right," he said tautly. "Not that I expect it to do much good. We'll have to wait and see how he reacts to your new image."

"I'll cross my fingers," she murmured.

"So will I. You'll need all the help you can get," he said flatly. "Let's go. I want to take you home and get back to work."

"Do you have to work all the time?" she asked involuntarily as they went out the door.

His jaw was taut, his eyes suddenly haunted. "If I want to stay sane, I do," he said curtly.

She stopped at the elevator and stared up at him. It was only because he was Denny's brother—stepbrother—that she was curious about him, she told herself.

"Because you miss her?" she asked softly, nodding toward the apartment.

He seemed to know immediately what she meant, but his face tightened dangerously. "I don't discuss Jessica,'' he said harshly. ''Not even with family, and you're damned sure not that. Not yet.''

Her face flamed at the rebuff. She hadn't expected the sheer savagery of it, and it almost brought tears to her eyes. She went into the elevator and not another word passed between them all the way back to her apartment.

The next week went by with merciful swiftness. Kenna spent it missing Denny and doing her best to avoid Regan. That wasn't possible. He spent his free time schooling her, tutoring her in the cold voice that she'd learned to hate. She resented him fiercely, and let him know it with every look, every word. The tension between them was almost visible, and she knew without words that he felt the same hostility she did. Their animosity was feeding on itself, and she found herself living for Denny's return.

Friday came finally, and Kenna breathed a sigh of relief as she gathered up her purse and coat to leave the office.

The door to Regan's office opened before she escaped, and he stood there with his jacket off, his shirt carelessly unbuttoned at the throat, his sleeves rolled up and his tie off, staring at her.

She didn't speak. She was trapped in that all-encompassing glance that took in her low-cut beige blouse with the pleated tan skirt and flashy polka-dotted scarf. Her makeup was perfect, and even with her glasses on, she was becoming enough to draw attention.

"Come here," he murmured, watching her.

She went to him involuntarily, her body swaying seductively, her eyes holding his, her steps sure and graceful. She stopped just in front of him, and watched the slow, sensuous smile that tugged at his chiseled, sensuous mouth.

"Nice," he murmured under his breath. "Very nice. I think you'll pass muster, Miss Dean. Which dress were you planning to wear tomorrow night—that sea-colored bit of witchery?"

"Yes," she agreed, her voice sounding breathless. She wondered why he was having this effect on her.

He nodded. "I'll pick you up at six-thirty. Denny's going to have a surprise and a half, isn't he?" he mused.

"He probably won't know me," she agreed, smiling.

"Just remember that you're supposed to belong to me," he reminded her curtly. "And don't fling yourself at his head at the first opportunity or you'll ruin everything."

She glared furiously. "I remember the game plan, counselor, I don't need constant reminding."

"You'll get it, nevertheless. I want this to work as much as you do," he reminded her. "The whole idea is to make Denny jealous. You'll only manage that if he thinks we're getting involved."

"Does that mean I have to look at you adoringly and bat my eyelashes in public?" she asked, her expression conveying distaste.

"That's exactly what it means," he agreed. "We'll have to put on a show in the office as well, if we're going to make him believe it."

"I will not sit on your lap to take dictation," she said shortly.

"What the hell makes you think I'd let you?" he asked, his eyes hard.

She turned around, clutching her purse in a stranglehold and made for the door just as it swung open and Denny came in, grinning.

He stopped short at the sight of Kenna, both eyebrows going up. "Well, well," he murmured, stunned.

Regan went up behind her, one arm sliding around her shoulders with seeming affection, and Kenna almost flinched at the unfamiliar touch of his warm, hard fingers.

"I wasn't expecting you until tomorrow," Regan told the younger man pleasantly. "You're taking Margo to the ball, I presume?"

"Uh-uh-uh—yes," Denny stammered, taking in the sight of his stepbrother apparently being affectionate with his secretary.

"Kenna was just going home," Regan continued. "You didn't plan to work this afternoon?"

"No," Denny managed.

"I'll see Kenna out, and then I'll fill you in on what's been happening while you were away. And you can tell me what you found out in New York." He tightened his grasp on Kenna, as if he were afraid she was going to make a grab for Denny. "I'll walk you out, love," he said.

She managed a wan smile in Denny's direction.

"Welcome home, boss," she called over her shoulder.

"Yes," he said in an odd voice. "Welcome home."

Regan purposely left the door ajar, aware of Denny's following gaze. He caught Kenna by the shoulders.

"I'll see you tomorrow at six-thirty," he told her, his deep voice sensuous, full of velvet. "Wear that sexy dress for me, baby," he added, and his eyes warned her to go along with him. He bent to her mouth and she let her eyes close, hating what was coming but powerless to move away. After all, the whole purpose of the exercise was to catch Denny's attention, to make him jealous.

Regan's mouth was hard and warm, and she barely felt its rough crush before he drew back and let her go. "I'll call you later," he told her, his eyes as cold as stone despite the deliberate warmth of his voice.

"Don't work too hard," she said, trying to infuse that same warmth in her own voice. She smiled half-heartedly and turned, walking quickly to the elevator.

Once she was inside it, she half-collapsed against the railing.

She felt strangely weak. It was seeing Denny again, she imagined, the sudden shock of seeing him when she hadn't expected to. Her fingers touched her mouth. She still felt the quick, hard pressure of Regan's lips, like a wound.

What if he were wrong? What if Denny didn't get jealous, what if he were too wrapped up in his precious Margo to care that Kenna was supposedly involving herself with Regan? She sighed. It would be just her luck to have the whole thing backfire. And if it did, she'd never forgive Regan.

Saturday night she dressed with special care, taking longer than usual with her makeup and leaving off her glasses. Who cared if she was half blind; Regan could just lead her around by the hand. That might be more convincing anyway, and he could describe Denny's expression to her.

He was on time, as usual, and she opened the door to find him in very conservative black evening clothes, with a white silk shirt emphasizing his darkness.

She squinted up at him. "Mr. Cole, I presume?" she asked.

"Can't you tell?" he asked, and she felt the impact of his eyes on her slender body. The dress left very little to the imagination.

"I don't need my glasses as long as I'm with someone," she returned, leaving him standing there while she went to find her purse and the black shawl she planned to wear with the dress. "All you have to do is steer me around open manholes."

"Your glasses look fine," he growled.

"That's tough, counselor, because I'm not wearing them tonight," she said antagonistically, whirling with skirts flying to confront him.

His face was only a pale blur, but she sensed his anger. "Let's go," he said shortly.

She followed him out the door without a word. She felt strangely vulnerable without her glasses, unprotected. But his bulk was reassuring, and she knew instinctively that she couldn't be more secure than in his company. He might not like her, but he'd take care of her.

He was quiet all the way to the hotel, and she didn't speak either. Strangely enough, her mind kept going back to the quick, hard kiss he'd crushed against her surprised lips outside the office. It wasn't the first time a man had kissed her, but it had made her feel odd. She didn't even like Regan, for heaven's sake, and she was in love with Denny, so why should that kiss have had such an impact on her? She forced herself not to think about it.

The ballroom boasted a live orchestra, and the colors of the women's gowns made a bright kaleidoscope. All Kenna saw were shapes and swirls of color, not individual faces, but it was enchanting and when she squinted she could recognize people. She found Denny and Margo immediately. They were standing by the punch bowl, smiling at each other, and she felt the color drain out of her face.

"Stop that," Regan said curtly. "You look like somebody's grandmother when you squint."

"Thank you, fairy godfather, for the coach and glass slippers," she returned, glaring in his general direction, "but now could you wave your magic wand and disappear?"

"Sorry, honey," he murmured, "there's nothing I'd like better, but circumstances dictate a different course. Act loving, you sweet little prude, and smile!"

She did, sickeningly, and clung to his hard arm as she caught a glimpse of Denny and Margo heading toward them. "My, my, how you do go on," she drawled. "And how I wish you would—go on, that is."

"Shut up, they're coming." He slid his arm around her waist. "Hello, Denny."

"Hi, big brother," came the pleasant reply. A thrill of pleasure went through Kenna at the sound of Denny's voice. "Who's this dishy thing with you?"

"As if you didn't know," Regan chuckled, hugging her close. "Kenna and I just got here."

Denny was close enough now that Kenna could see his shocked features as he studied her. "What happened to you?" he mumbled "You look . . . different."

"I happened to her," Regan said, his tone threatening enough to catch his brother's attention.

"Well, well," Denny muttered, "and I thought you two were likely to kill each other if I left you alone for a week."

"May I be introduced?" the dark-eyed, raven-haired woman at Denny's side asked gently.

"Oh, excuse me, of course! Margo de la Vera, this is my stepbrother, Regan Cole, and my secretary, Kenna Dean."

Regan caught the woman's hand and raised it to his lips with devastating finesse. *"Señorita, mucho gusto en conocerla,"* he said in perfect Spanish.

Taken aback, the full-lipped woman smiled widely. *"Con mucho gusto, señor. Habla usted español?"*

"Un poco," he agreed, smiling back. "Denny has good taste."

"No, *señor,* it is I who have that," Margo said softly, and her eyes openly worshipped Denny. She was unexpectedly gracious, smiling even at Kenna, her eyes gentle, friendly.

Kenna, who had seen Margo in the office several times but had never spoken to her, had expected a cold, icy veneer with a money-hungry heart under it. This woman was totally unexpected.

"I'm very pleased to meet you," Kenna managed with a wan smile. Margo was only a year or so older than she was, but possessed far more maturity and poise.

"And I, you," Margo replied, nodding. "Denny says that the office would surely fall apart without you."

"How kind of him," Kenna mumbled.

"How honest of him," Regan chuckled, drawing her closer. "She keeps our noses to the grindstone, don't you, honey?"

Denny was frowning now, puzzled. "Would you like to dance, Kenna?" he asked suddenly.

Kenna's heart leapt up and she was opening her lips to accept when Regan shook his head and his fingers bit into her waist. "Sorry," he told his stepbrother with dangerously glittering eyes. "She's booked for the night, I'm afraid."

Denny looked uncomfortable, but he quickly erased the expression from his face and caught Margo's hand. "I don't blame you, the way she looks," he told Regan. "Well, we'll go sway to the beat some more. See you later."

"Come by my place about midnight and we'll have a nightcap," Regan told them.

"We'd like that," Denny said, drawing Margo along with him.

"Oh, damn you," Kenna spat at Regan the first chance she got, as he was pushing her around the ballroom to a waltz.

"Your one chance to be in Denny's arms," he laughed mockingly, "and I cheated you out of it, is that what you're thinking? Well, honey, no man wants what's openly on offer. The harder it is to come by, the more he wants it."

Her face closed up and she dropped her gaze to his shirt-front, fixing it involuntarily on Denny and Margo as they waltzed past. Margo, in her peach-colored gown, with her dark coloring was strikingly beautiful. It wasn't hard to see why Denny was so attracted to her. Even with her new trappings, Kenna felt inferior to her.

"She's beautiful, isn't she?" she asked Regan. "And not the cold, mercenary woman you assumed."

"Appearances can be deceiving, honey," he reminded her. "I've seen innocent little things who were as cold as cash registers in bed."

"Do you have to buy your women, counselor?" she asked with an oversweet smile.

His eyes glittered down at her. "You'll pay for that one," he said quietly.

"I'm shaking in my size eight shoes," she assured him. "Isn't it lucky for me that we're in this crowd?"

"Enjoy it while you can."

"I would, if you'd let me dance with Denny," she grumbled.

"I know what I'm doing, even if you don't," he said, whirling her around. His arm suddenly drew her tight against him, and she started at the close contact with his long, powerful legs.

The involuntary little gasp was something she couldn't help. The feel of him was like a brand, and she tried to draw back.

His arm only tightened until her breasts were crushed softly against his jacket. "Will you relax?" he growled. "Denny's glaring in this direction; I'd like to give him something to think about."

"Oh!" she exclaimed, and let him fold her closer. The feel of his big, hard body at close quarters was doing strange things to her equilibrium. She felt light-headed, shaky. She must be tired, she told herself.

"That's it," he murmured over her head, "just let go, let your body rest against mine.

Dancing is like making love, you have to let the man lead.''

She flushed to the roots of her hair and stiffened, until the caressing movements of his hand made her give in again.

"You haven't danced much, have you?" he asked quietly. "You flinch every time your thighs brush mine, as if even this kind of intimacy is new to you."

It was, but she wouldn't admit it to her worst enemy. Her fingers clutched at his lapels, and they felt like ice, numb with nervousness. She didn't dare look up. It was bad enough that his cologne was invading her senses, that the warm maleness of him was wrapping around her and sapping her strength. She couldn't risk meeting his eyes at point-blank range. He frightened her too much.

"Don't stiffen up, darling," he whispered, and his fingers curled into hers seductively. "Let go. Let me feel you."

He was drowning her in new sensations. She knew what he was doing, he was using his expertise to seduce her so that Denny would think there was something between them. But her body was being tricked into responding to his, and her mind couldn't protect it anymore.

Her thighs, when they met his, trembled wildly, and she caught her breath when his hand slid down low on her back to bring her hips completely against his.

"Oh, no, don't!" she whispered shakenly, tugging against his hand.

His head bent so that his breath was on her ear, and he nipped the lobe with his teeth. His own breath was strangely harsh, quick. "Don't you know what I'm doing?" he asked.

"Yes," she agreed in a stranger's voice. "But..."

"Don't read anything personal into it," he murmured gruffly. "We're putting on a show, that's all. You're vulnerable to this kind of intimacy because you're a virgin. It would be the same with any experienced man."

Would it? She almost voiced the question, and her own thoughts shocked her. The way she was reacting to him was dangerous, but she couldn't help it. Her senses were screaming for something she'd never experienced, wanting a closer contact than this, wanting something...more.

"Regan?" she whispered shakily.

His breath seemed to catch at the unfamiliar sound of his name on her lips. "What?"

"Please...don't hold me like this," she pleaded. Her fingers crushed the lapel of his jacket. "It frightens me."

He drew in a slow, deep breath and loosened his tight hold. "Why?" he asked.

She couldn't tell him that. She didn't know herself. But she sighed with relief when he let her move slightly away. Something had been happening to him, too, something she wasn't familiar with, a rigidity that was unmistakable.

"Isn't the music lovely?" she asked nervously.

His fingers moved caressingly on hers. "A man's body can play tricks on him," he whispered at her ear. "It doesn't necessarily take the feel of a woman against him to trigger it, either."

She flushed wildly and wondered if she could pull loose and run without attracting too much attention.

"It wasn't that," she choked.

"Wasn't it?" He drew back and looked down into her stunned eyes. "If you could see your face," he murmured with a strange smile. "Did it shock you?"

She tore her eyes from his with a tiny cry. "Don't," she whispered.

"Virgin," he murmured quietly. His fingers contracted violently around hers for an instant, and she thought she felt his cheek brush softly against her hair.

She swallowed down her nervousness and managed a shaky laugh. "Don't get any ideas about offering me up as a sacrifice, will you?"

He laughed softly beside her forehead. "Those cultures died out years ago. Have you ever seen the pyramids in Mexico and Central America?"

That brought her eyes up quickly. "And in Peru? Oh, I'd give anything to climb all over them," she said without reservation. "I wanted to go into archaeology, but I didn't have the money to pursue graduate courses...."

Something had shadowed his eyes for an instant as he stared down at her. "I'll have to show you my collection of photos one of these days," he murmured. "I took an archaeology tour a couple of years back and saw all those places."

Her face brightened with mingled pleasure and surprise. "Well, well, who'd have thought it?'' she murmured. ''I didn't think you old fossils liked other old fossils.''

His eyebrows went straight up. ''Flirting with me, Miss Dean?'' he asked in an odd tone.

She'd forgotten for an instant that he was the enemy. She turned her eyes to Denny, and a pang of regret went through her as she saw him bend his blond head to listen to Margo's animated chatter. The sadness showed in her face and Regan reacted to it violently, his arm crushing her against him for an instant.

''Stop it,'' he growled. ''Must you wear your heart on your sleeve?''

''It's not working,'' she muttered miserably, staring at his shirt front, at the quick rise and fall of it. ''He wouldn't notice me if I danced a flamenco nude.''

''Give it time, honey,'' he said. ''You can't expect everything at once.''

''So they say.'' She was glad when the music ended. Dancing with Regan was disturbing, and she was relieved to break contact with his hard body.

As it turned out, she didn't manage even one dance with Denny, although the hope of it kept her beaming all evening. But at eleven thirty, when Regan gestured for her to join him, she was forced to give up. Apparently, what Regan had said to him at the beginning of the ball had kept Denny from even asking her to dance. Head down, she went to the door, her evening bag clutched in her hand, and let Regan lead her out into the night.

Chapter Five

Regan seemed preoccupied with his own thoughts and hardly said a word on the way back. Kenna sat rigidly beside him, feeling odd and unfamiliar sensations and disliking them and him acutely.

Why hadn't he let her dance with Denny just once? It wouldn't have mattered so much, and she would have lived on it all her life. Her eyes closed on a wave of pain. Denny was so obviously wrapped up in his South American paramour. How did a plain little country girl go about fighting that kind of beauty and sophistication? Oh, she'd drawn his eye, thanks to Regan's coaching. But it took more than physical attraction to make a relationship work. She wanted more than that from Denny. So much more!

"Take off the glass slippers, honey," Regan said with a bite in his voice as he parked the car in the garage beneath his apartment building. "It's almost midnight."

She opened her eyes with a sigh. "Are we here?" she murmured, glancing around at the dark blurs of other cars.

"You little bat," he grumbled. "If you'd wear your glasses, you could see for yourself."

"This is much nicer," she countered, opening the door for herself before he could do it for her. "I don't have to see you, do I?" she added with a cold smile.

She caught the flash of his eyes before he slammed the car door behind her and locked it. "Don't push your luck, Kenna," he said curtly.

It was one of the few times he'd ever used her name, and the sound rippled through her like tumbling water. She tossed her head, and suddenly she missed the former length of her hair. Her hand went to it, rumpling the waves.

"I miss my hair," she murmured, following him into the elevator.

"Well, I don't," he growled, and lit another cigarette. He was setting new records tonight, he'd smoked so many. He glanced at her head. "At least it doesn't look like barbed wire now."

"Do, please, say what you think," she said with biting sarcasm, glaring up at the hazy features of his hard face. Her wide, bright eyes searched his in the silence; she could hardly make them out without squinting. But she wasn't going to squint. She looked away.

"I always do," he returned coldly. The elevator door opened and he led the way to his apartment, unlocking it with a minimum of motion and then standing aside so she could enter first.

He turned on the lights and went straight to the bar. He poured himself a whiskey, a big one, and took a long sip before he glanced her way.

"Would you like sherry or a brandy?" he asked curtly.

"I am allowed to drink hard liquor," she said, her eyes flashing. "Or do I look like a milk fanatic?"

"Whiskey would go to your head," he replied. He poured an inch of brandy into a snifter and set it on the coffee table in front of the sofa, where she was perched on the very edge of the seat. "Can you see it?" he asked with a mocking smile, "or would you like me to shove it under your nose?"

"I'd like to tell you where to shove it," she flashed back at him, feeling herself bristling, sparring with him, wanting to fight. Needing it.

"Go ahead," he invited, draining his glass. He set it roughly on the coffee table in front of her.

"You are so smug," she accused. She took a sip of the brandy, grimaced, and put it back down. Her indulgence in alcohol was limited to wine on special occasions, and, blissfully unaware of its age and excellence, she didn't appreciate the fiery taste of the brandy. "Re-arranging people's lives for them, deciding whom they should marry," she continued, her face livid with anger and wounded pride and disappointment. "Who pulls your strings, Mr. Famous Attorney, the ghost you live with?"

He went rigid. Absolutely rigid, and it was as well that she couldn't see the dangerous glitter in his eyes. It probably wouldn't have stopped her, anyway.

"It's all right for you to pull my appearance to pieces and order Denny's life for him, but nobody discusses your life, do they?" she continued, rising from the sofa. "What's so secretive about your late wife that you can't even discuss her without exploding, Mr. Cole? Was she trying to get away from you when she died . . . oh!"

The sheer fury of his sudden movement cut her off in mid-sentence. She felt his hands grasping, hurting, as he slammed her down onto the sofa and pinned her there with the impact of his big, warm body.

"Damn you," he growled as he took her mouth, hurting her, grinding his lips into it until she felt his teeth cutting her lower lip. "Damn you to hell . . ."

She could hardly breathe for the weight of him, and she was afraid of a man for the first time in her life, physically afraid. His hands were inhumanly strong as they pinned her wrists into the cushions above her head, his chest hurt as it ground down against her soft breasts. There was a tautness to his powerful body that threatened, and his physical superiority was both evident and terrifying.

Tears were stinging her eyes as his mouth bit hers, twisting angrily, hurting and meaning to hurt, as if he were taking out his anguish on her defenseless body.

She had no idea how far he might go, and she knew that she couldn't stop him. She stiffened, closing her eyes against the fleeting glimpse of his furious scowl, the dark passion in his face. She moaned piteously against his rough mouth, breathing in its smoky warmth as she tried to get enough air to breathe.

The sound seemed to get through to him, along with the tears he could taste on her face.

He lifted his dark head, breathing roughly and much too fast, and looked into her frightened eyes. His mouth made a straight line when he saw her pale face, her swollen lips, her tear-reddened eyes.

"My wife," he breathed unsteadily, "was six months pregnant with our baby when she died. She was flying to meet me in Charleston when the plane went down."

She felt her eyes burn with new tears. She ached for him, for the hurt she read in his steady gaze, for the pain he must have suffered. It would have been bad enough to lose a woman he loved. But to lose her like that, to lose his child with her. . . .

Her body relaxed all at once. She searched his face. "I'm sorry," she said softly, and all the anger and fear and pain went out of her with the words. "I'm so very sorry, Regan."

His face contorted. "I loved her," he breathed roughly, the words torn from him. "Three years, three long, lonely years."

His body relaxed, too, although he didn't move. He looked down at her steadily, curiously. "I hurt you," he murmured, as if he was only just realizing it.

Her tongue touched the place his teeth had damaged. "It's all right," she whispered. "I deserved that, and you know it. I never dreamed I could hurt anyone deliberately. . . ."

His eyes dropped to the swollen lip. "We're even, then," he said quietly. "Because I've never been that rough with a woman in my life."

Her breath was still coming far too quickly, and she was becoming slowly aware of new sensations in her slender body. Her breasts were tautening, swelling, and the dress had slid away until one of them was all but bare to the sudden interest in his dark eyes.

She felt her body tremble suddenly, knowing that he could feel it, too, couldn't help but feel it. His eyes slid back up to search hers before they fell to her soft, trembling mouth.

His head bent again, wordlessly, and his mouth brushed softly against hers. His tongue drew a slow pattern over her swollen lower lip, healing, tantalizing, his breath smoky and faintly unsteady.

He stretched her, his hands tugging gently at hers to draw her body to its full length even as he covered it fully with his own. She felt his hips pressing firmly over hers, and the same thing that had happened to him while they danced was happening again.

She stiffened under him, and his lips poised just above hers.

"No, don't do that," he said softly, his voice almost unrecognizable, because it was tender. "I won't hurt you." His hands, where they held hers, became slowly caressing. His mouth brushed down over hers in a tingling parody of a kiss. "Lie still," he breathed against her lips. "Despite what you've heard about men, most of us aren't that dangerous when we're hungry.''

The very calmness of his tone eased the tension out of her. She didn't understand why she wasn't fighting, or demanding to be let loose. The feel of his body was intoxicating, all warm muscle and strength. He was bigger than she'd realized, her arms would barely have reached around that broad chest. She shifted involuntarily, and he eased his hips to one side, so that only his chest was pinning her to the soft cushions.

Her eyes looked straight up into his, curious and searching. He returned the frank stare, without blinking. ''You're very soft,'' he breathed.

Her lips parted. ''You're...enormous,'' she managed. She studied the broad, quiet face poised over her own, fascinated by its hard lines. It was as if she'd never really looked at him.

''What are you staring at so hard?'' he murmured.

''Your nose,'' she confessed. ''It's been broken.''

''Twice,'' he agreed, and smiled faintly. ''I served in Nam, in the Marines.''

She wanted to touch that formidable nose, his mouth. "Would you let go of my hands?" she asked.

He released them, to slide his own hands under her back, where the dress left it bare. Her fingers moved up to his face, hesitating.

"It's all right," he said softly. "I don't mind being touched."

Her fingers ran over his nose, where the break had been, and over his cheeks. He was clean-shaven, but there was already a trace of stubble. His chin was square and his heavy brows jutted over his deep-set eyes. There were faint lines at the corners of his eyes, and he had traces of silver tangling in the hair at his temples.

He bent, nuzzling her nose with his, so close now that her eyes could hardly see him. "Your eyes have gold flecks in them," he murmured.

"Yours don't," she whispered back, framing his face with her hands to hold it away. "They're very nearly black."

"My French ancestry," he said. His eyes narrowed. "Still afraid of me, Kenna?"

Her lips parted. "No," she said, and her own reply shocked her. But she wasn't afraid of him. Not anymore.

His finger touched her lips and his eyes fell to it. "That's interesting," he said, "because I think I'm afraid of you."

"Why?" she asked involuntarily.

"Virgins make me nervous," he murmured, with a wicked smile. "I suppose you'd faint if I eased that witchy gown down around your waist and looked at you, wouldn't you?"

She felt her cheeks catch fire. "Yes, I probably would," she admitted.

He frowned slightly. "You're damned inexperienced, do you know that?"

"Yes," she said, grimacing. "Well, the way I look...looked...who'd want to teach me anything?" she added bitterly.

"The way you look right now, who wouldn't?" he mused. He propped himself over her so that his breath was warm on her lips. "You need a little educating, Miss Dean," he breathed, "for your own sake. It takes experience to make a woman seductive."

She swallowed, once again shockingly aware of the message his body was sending out. "That depends on what kind of education you have in mind."

He smiled wickedly as his mouth brushed over her eyelids, closing them. "Nothing traumatic, little nun," he murmured. "Just some remedial lovemaking."

Before she could find an answer to that blatant observation, his mouth was on hers. She stiffened for an instant at the intimacy. It wasn't unpleasant now; he wasn't trying to hurt. His lips were patient and very gentle. She barely felt them. But as the pressure began to deepen and the pleasant brushing turned to hunger, her eyes opened and looked up. His own eyes were closed, his brows drawn together in something like pain. His lashes were thick as brushes, and dark as night where they lay on his cheek. She closed her own eyes again, strangely touched.

One arm slid under her, and she felt his fingers just at the outer edge of her breast, lightly brushing. Not intimate, but oddly arousing, causing sensations she'd never felt.

His mouth lifted for an instant. "How sore is that lip?" he asked in a deep whisper.

Her eyes lazily came open. "What?" she murmured, drunk on pleasure.

He laughed softly. "Never mind." He bent again, lifting a hand to catch her jaw and open her mouth gently. "Now leave it like this," he breathed as his own mouth opened and fitted itself to hers exactly.

She caught her breath at the new intimacy. She felt his tongue exploring her inner lip, darting into her mouth, and she gasped at the sensual feel of it. Her fingers bit into his arms and trembled.

He raised his head, scowling. "You are a little nun, aren't you?" he asked under his breath. "It's called a French kiss," he told her, searching her wide eyes. "Men like it."

Her eyes went to her own fingers, digging into his hard, muscled arms. "I...I think I like it too," she admitted, meeting his eyes again. "No one ever kissed me like that, Regan."

"I'm beginning to realize that no one ever did much of anything to you," he replied. His eyes searched hers quietly. "Have you been lonely for a long time, Cinderella?" he asked suddenly.

The question startled her, because it was so close to the truth, and tears stung her eyes.

"Don't," he said softly, and bent to brush the tears away with his mouth. "Don't. I know what loneliness is. I know how it feels."

Yes, he knew, probably better than she ever would, and she ached to take that horrible pain out of his eyes. Her fingers moved up to smooth away the hair at his temples.

He kissed her face tenderly, touching every soft inch of it. "The nights are the worst, aren't they?" he breathed. "Going to a movie and watching couples hold hands, seeing families grouped together in restaurants—oh, yes, I know what it's like."

"There's a difference," she murmured, feeling so safe with him, now, so strangely in tune with him. "Men can ask women out."

He lifted his free hand to touch her face. "And you can't?" He smiled gently at the expression on her delicate features. "It's allowed these days."

She shifted restlessly. "And men get the wrong idea, don't they? Or rather, the right idea, because most girls don't care."

"That," he sighed, "is a fact. I'm pretty old-fashioned myself, Cinders. I don't like being chased."

"Are you . . . chased?" she asked.

He nodded. "I'm rich, haven't you noticed?"

She shook her head and smiled. "I was too busy noticing your big feet and your broken nose ... oh, no fair!'' she gasped when he dug her in the ribs.

He chuckled down at her. ''Salaaming at my door ... I was in a rotten mood that morning, I felt like sitting on you.''

She smiled back. ''I'm glad you didn't, my hospitalization policy doesn't cover damage done by irate bosses.''

''What a sharp little tongue.'' He moved down, and something new and exciting glittered in his dark eyes as they studied her mouth. ''Do you know what to do with it now?'' he asked.

Even as he spoke, he touched his mouth to hers, and smiled as it opened and her tongue repeated the wild little caress his had taught her.

His breath came quick and rough, and his free hand moved to her throat. ''Again,'' he whispered against her lips. ''Don't stop just when you're getting the hang of it.''

She lifted her arms around his neck and gave in to him, sharing a kiss that made her toes curl with pure pleasure as her tongue met his and fenced with it. Seconds later, she felt his hand easing down to brush lightly at the soft curve of her breast. The other hand was under her arm, lightly teasing, and between the two of them, she felt her body go taut with something strained and threatening.

She caught her breath and he lifted his dark head to watch her.

I should stop you, she told herself as she drowned in those dark eyes and reveled in the tantalizing seduction of his hands as they played around the edges of her breast. But she was curious and blazing with unexpected hungers. Involuntarily her body arched and twisted to invite his hands inside the thin dress.

"Your eyes are the shade of budding leaves," he whispered, looking into them, "in a spring mist. I could get lost in them. That's it, honey, lift up for me."

"Please," she whispered, shaken.

"Not yet," he replied, his voice, his eyes, tender, his hands tormenting, until what she felt bordered on anguish. "Not until you want it more than breath."

"Do you want me . . . to beg?" she moaned.

"No," he whispered. "I want you to need it. I want you to need me. I want to make it the sweetest pleasure you've ever known."

She arched again, dragging at breath, staring straight into his dark eyes the whole time while her body caught fire and burned. "What are you doing to me?" she moaned helplessly.

"Taking possession," he breathed, and even as he spoke, his hand slowly moved, moving inside the bodice to cup her, to press against taut, swelling flesh.

It was so sweet that she cried out, tears swimming in her eyes, brimming, as she bit her lip at the tiny, delicious consummation and clung to him, burying her face against his shoulder.

"You see?" he whispered, cradling her small breast gently. "You can't rush it. It has to be slow to be good."

She trembled in his embrace, feeling him turn so that she was lying beside him, against him, without the enforced intimacy of his body.

Without knowing why, she began to cry. His arms swallowed her, meeting behind her back, and he held her, rocking her softly, his cheek on her dark hair.

"I'm sorry," she whispered, shaken, "I don't know what's the matter with me."

His hand smoothed her hair, gentling her. "I'm the one who should be apologizing," he murmured. "I didn't mean to hurt you, Kenna."

"I know that," she whispered into his shoulder. "I don't know why I said those horrible things to you...."

"Probably for the same reason I've been saying them to you, but this isn't the time or the place to hash it out." He sighed and stretched lazily. "Feel better?"

"That's a leading question," she replied, sitting up. She glanced down at him and blushed.

He chuckled at the expression on her face. "What a revealing color. Scarlet, isn't it?"

She made a harsh sound and scrambled over his long legs to get to her feet. She grabbed up the brandy snifter and drained it, hardly aware of the taste.

"Kenna . . ." he began.

She put the snifter down. "Uh, Denny and Margo should be here soon, shouldn't they?" she asked, suddenly nervous and uncertain.

He got up, too, and moved in front of her to take her gently but firmly by the shoulders. He tilted her face up to his searching eyes.

"I'll never hurt you again," he said quietly. "That's a promise. Don't start getting self-conscious with me because I lost my head for a minute.''

''I'm self-conscious because I lost mine,'' she confessed, avoiding his gaze.

''That should have happened to you years ago,'' he said quietly. ''Some very lucky man should have shown you what it was all about.''

Her eyes fell to his chest. ''No one ever wanted to,'' she admitted miserably. She glanced up at him, aching. ''Was it pity tonight?''

''My God, no!'' he burst out. His hands tightened on her arms. ''If you want the truth, I suppose I wanted to make amends for hurting you. But it wasn't out of pity, or misplaced compassion.''

Her eyes searched his. ''Were you pretending that I was her?'' she asked, nodding toward the small framed photo.

He scowled darkly. ''I don't play that kind of game,'' he replied coldly. ''I loved my wife, but I didn't climb in the grave with her, and I don't need substitutes. Does that answer your question?'' He released her all at once and moved away to light a cigarette.

She stared at his broad back, remembering how the warm muscles had felt against her hands. It mattered, that he hadn't pretended she was Jessica while he was kissing her. She didn't understand why, but it mattered very much.

"I'm sorry," she said helplessly. "I seem to make a habit of sticking my foot in my mouth lately."

He turned, his eyes holding hers. "Don't you know why we strike sparks off each other? Aren't you even mature enough to understand that?"

Her tongue touched the small bruise on her lower lip, and he followed the movement with his eyes. "Yes," she admitted, feeling raw. "I understand why."

He took a long drag on the cigarette, but he didn't look away. "In that case, you'll also understand if I tell you that we're going to have to tone it down and start getting along with each other. Denny's the object of the chase, not me."

She blushed red. "I hadn't forgotten," she replied with equal coldness.

His eyes went up and down her body, lingering on her bodice, and she knew that he was remembering, as she was, the feel of skin against skin.

"It should have been Denny, shouldn't it?" he asked bitterly. He laughed mirthlessly as he lifted the cigarette to his chiseled mouth. "Well, there'll be other firsts for him." His head jerked as the sound of the doorbell suddenly exploded into the strained silence. "Just in time."

He went to open the door, leaving Kenna to stare blankly after him.

It wasn't until Denny and Margo walked in the door that Kenna realized how she must look. Denny was close enough that she could make out his expression, and there was open curiosity in it as he added her ruffled hair and swollen lips to Regan's equally ruffled hair and lipstick-smeared mouth.

"Had you forgotten you invited us?" Denny asked Regan, and there was a note in his voice that Kenna had never heard him use with the older man.

"Not at all," Regan said smoothly. "What can I get you to drink?"

"Bourbon, straight, for me," Denny said coolly. "Margo, what would you like?"

"I prefer cognac, if you have it," the other woman replied, studying Denny with eyes that suddenly went from affectionate to angry.

"Kenna?" Regan asked, barely glancing her way as he went to the bar.

"Another brandy, please," she murmured, handing him her snifter.

"Well, how did you like the ball, Kenna?" Denny asked, moving close to study her small, wounded face.

"It was very nice," she managed.

"I also enjoyed it," Margo said, moving to Denny's side to grasp his arm possessively. She hugged him close, her eyes warning Kenna off.

"What happened to your lip?" Denny asked curtly, glancing toward Regan.

"None of your damned business," Regan said in a dangerously soft tone as he handed the drinks around.

Denny's eyes narrowed as he grasped the glass in one hand. "That could change very easily," he replied.

Regan lifted his own glass in a mock toast. "*Nolo contendere,* counselor," he said.

Kenna watched Denny's face flush angrily as he recognized the legal phrase which meant *no contest.*

Denny finished his drink and Margo sipped at hers, while Regan sidetracked his step-brother into a discussion of a case they were working on. But the tension was still there fifteen minutes later, when Denny suddenly announced that he and Margo had to leave.

Margo had said hardly two words to Kenna, her whole posture defensive and jealous. Kenna disliked her possessive attitude, but wasn't as upset by it as she would have expected. And that was puzzling, too. She felt confused.

Kenna escaped to the powder room to get away from the emotional undercurrents, and when she came back, Denny and Margo were gone.

Regan stood quietly in the center of the living room, turning as Kenna joined him.

"You'll be delighted to hear that Denny was prepared to commit mayhem on your behalf," he said pleasantly, raising his glass in a salute.

She blinked. "Why?"

He moved close and touched her lower lip with his forefinger. "Because of that," he said. "He thinks I was manhandling you."

"With reason, I'm afraid," she reminded him. "Did you tell Denny why...?"

"And spoil his disgusting suspicions? I did not." He drained the glass and set it down on the bar. "I'd sleep with my doors locked, if I were you. Margo's sweet disposition went into eclipse."

"I noticed that," she said with a faint smile. "Denny was really worried?" she persisted, brightening.

"He was worried," he said, his tone harsh. "I'd better get you home. It's late."

"You could call a cab," she suggested, moving to pick up her shawl and purse from the sofa.

"You're not going home alone," he said firmly. "No city is that safe."

She took one look at his set features and decided not to argue. He was quite capable of carrying her down to the lobby.

He drove her home without speaking, keeping the radio on to fill the silence. Her eyes darted to his grim face, as she tried to reconcile the hostile, taciturn man she worked for with the ardent, expert lover who could have carried her unprotesting to his bed less than an hour before. She could still taste him on her lips, feel the tender brush of his fingers on her bare skin. The sensations memory aroused shocked her. She hardly recognized the passionate woman who'd begged for his hands on

her untouched body. So much for her fine
principles. They'd collapsed at the first temp-
tation. All at once, she wondered how it would
have been with Denny and was surprised to
find that she couldn't imagine being touched
that way by the man she was supposedly in
love with.

They stood apart on the elevator, and he
glared at the closed doors as if they stood between him and salvation. Not one word passed
his lips all the way to the door of her apartment.

She was bending down to the doorknob trying to see where to put the key when he took it
away from her with a disgusted sound.

"If you'd wear your damned glasses, you'd
be able to see where to put the key, you blind
little bat," he growled.

"I could tell you where to put the key," she
returned hotly, straightening to glare up in his
general direction.

"Go ahead," he invited.

She drew in a steadying breath. "Good
night, counselor," she said.

"Good? Not very, Cinderella." he replied
shortly. "You lost Prince Charming somewhere along the way."

"And ended up with the beast," she shot back.

He stared down at her, and she caught a glimpse of aching loneliness in his hard face before he quickly erased it. "Story of my life," he murmured half-humorously. "Good night, Cinders."

He turned and walked away, and tears burned her eyes. She started to call to him, just as the elderly little woman down the hall opened her door and came out to take her garbage to the chute. Kenna sighed and turned back into her lonely apartment.

She made herself a cup of hot cocoa and paced the living room while she drank it. What was the matter with her, for heaven's sake? Why should she feel so miserable about calling Regan a beast? He was a beast!

A beast. She sighed. Sure, a beast who'd bent over backwards to help her improve her appearance, to act slinky and seductive and sophisticated so that she could attract Denny. And tonight she'd attracted Denny, and that didn't matter nearly so much as the fact that she'd deliberately gone out of her way to hurt Regan. That crack about his late wife had been utterly horrible. No wonder he couldn't bear to talk about it.

She moved toward the phone and stared angrily down at it. He was probably asleep already, this was insane! But all the same, her fingers searched through the telephone directory for his number and dialed it.

Her hand clenched around the still warm mug of hot cocoa while the phone rang once, twice, three times....

"Hello?" came a familiar, gruff voice over the line.

She opened her mouth and tried to speak, failed, and cleared her throat. "Regan?" she murmured.

There was a pause. "Kenna?" he asked softly.

"I don't think you're a beast at all," she said with equal softness and put the receiver down.

She stared at it for a long moment before she put down the mug, turned out the lights and went to bed.

Chapter Six

Sunday promised to be an ordeal. Kenna came home from church in no particular hurry, with nothing more to look forward to than more of her own company. She wandered down the street, staring up at the tall skyscrapers, her eyes drifting to the occasional oasis of trees that graced downtown Atlanta. It was odd how the downtown area had a suburban feeling to it. She constantly ran into people she knew, like the secretaries in the offices below hers and the owner of the small grocery store on the ground floor of her apartment building and the manager of the small boutique which was also among the businesses located there. It wasn't as lonely an existence as she'd once thought it might be when she moved to Atlanta from the small town where she'd grown up.

She dragged her feet, drinking in the sweet spring air, watching buds just beginning to pop out on the tall oak and maple trees, and the smaller dogwoods. The dogwoods would be in full blossom before too long, just in time for the city festival that bore their name.

With a final wistful sigh at the sight of a couple holding hands and sitting on a stretch of concrete bench along the street, she went into her apartment building. At least she felt good today, in her new lavender and white patterned dress, with its full skirt and neatly ruffled little neckline and puffy sleeves. She felt young and womanly all at once, gorgeous, a model. She made a leap into the elevator, whirling to push the button for her floor. She leaned dreamily back against the rail. Glasses or no glasses, old girl, you have got something, she told herself. She grinned. Confidence, perhaps. Maybe that accounted for this buoyant feeling. When she got to her apartment, she'd clean out her closet and get rid of those dowdy old clothes she'd been wearing for the past two years. That ought to keep her occupied.

The elevator stopped and she danced off it, her skirts flying against her long, lovely legs as she turned toward her apartment. She stopped so suddenly that she almost fell forward, and her heart jumped into her throat.

Regan was leaning back against the wall, brooding again, his eyes staring straight ahead at her door. One hand was in the pocket of his gray slacks, the other was holding a smoking cigarette. He was wearing a blue blazer with an open-necked white shirt, and his hair was rumpled...and it suddenly occurred to Kenna that she was falling in love with him. The discovery froze her where she stood. That notion had to go, and quickly, she told her heart. No mutinies around here, not when she was about to catch Denny's eye and live happily ever after. Cinderella didn't fall in love with the fairy godfather, it wasn't allowed.

As if he sensed her uneasy scrutiny, Regan's head turned and he stared at her. He was a good three doors away from where she was standing, but he might have been beside her. Her heart ran wild.

He straightened up as she forced her legs to carry her to him, and he smiled. And all at once, the sun came out and everything burst into glorious bloom.

"Hi," he murmured, giving her the once-over.

"Hi," she replied, sounding breathless.

"I thought you might be at loose ends. I'm driving down to see my parents. I thought you might like to come with me. Denny and Margo are going to be there," he added with a careless smile.

Something froze in blossom, but she erased the coldness from her eyes and smiled. "I'd like that very much. Should I change?"

"That's up to you. Personally," he murmured, studying her closely, "I like you this way."

"I might need a sweater," she said, unlocking her door. "I won't be a minute. Want to come in?"

He shook his head, disappointing her. "I'll wait out here. I don't expect it's going to take that long, is it?"

"No, of course not," she said quickly, and rushed in to get her sweater. Apparently he didn't want to be alone with her for any length of time unless they were in a car, and that suited her fine. Why should she want to risk a repeat of last night, after all? And Denny was the quarry, not Regan. She repeated that to herself as she tugged a white sweater from her closet, ran a comb through her hair, and hurried back to him.

"Does Denny know we're coming?" she asked Regan when they were inside the Porsche and speeding north toward Gainesville, where his father and stepmother lived.

He laughed softly. "Yes, he knows we're coming," he murmured, glancing toward her. "So does Margo, worse luck. I hope you're up to it, darling; you'll need your wits around that lady."

Darling! Why did the sound of that casual endearment on his lips make her heart run double-time? She shifted restlessly in the seat.

"What would you have done if I hadn't been home?" she asked.

"Checked the hospitals," he murmured, tongue-in-cheek.

"Thanks so much, you do wonders for my self-esteem," she grumbled, and her lips pouted.

He cocked an eyebrow. "Broke the truce, did I? All right, I'll reform. You look lovely, Miss Dean, and if you weren't hot and bothered by my stepbrother, I think I'd park this car and kiss you until you couldn't think straight."

She found it extremely hard to breathe after that rash admission. In her lap, she had a stranglehold on her purse. "Would you?" she asked in a high-pitched tone.

"Yes," he said shortly, "I would. And you'd let me."

Her eyes darted out the window to escape his. She didn't say anything because she couldn't.

"Why did you call me last night?" he asked harshly.

"Because I felt ashamed of myself," she ground out. "I always seem to say the wrong thing to you, at the wrong time. You've gone out of your way to help me, and I've done nothing but fight you."

He crushed out the cigarette he'd been smoking. "I've made you fight me," he said after a minute. "I put your back up the day I walked into the office, and I've done my damnedest to keep it that way."

The confession startled her. She half turned in her seat and stared at him across the console. "Why?"

He met her gaze levelly as he stopped at an intersection. "You know why," he said coldly.

Her face flamed as he said the words, and she couldn't have looked away from him to save her life. It was the most curious sensation, like being shocked. A jolt of electricity seemed to have surged from his vibrant body to hers.

"Kenna," he growled. They were on a county road, with no traffic anywhere around them. All at once he reached out, catching her by the back of the head, and pulled her mouth under his. "Come here, damn it," he muttered. The kiss was a wild sharing of mouths and tongues that blazed up like a forest fire in the sudden stillness.

His hand released the steering wheel to catch her under the arms and lift her as close as he could get her, despite the bucket seats and the confined space. Her breasts were crushed against his blue blazer, and his mouth hurt, a sweet, aching hurt that she wanted more than air.

He drew away a minute later, his breath shuddering against her lips. His eyes were glazed with desire, as she knew her own must be, because she wanted him suddenly, shockingly.

His nostrils flared as he searched her face, blind to the pickup truck crossing the intersection to the right of them, its occupants openly curious.

"I want you," he said curtly, putting it into words.

"I know," she whispered, her voice breathless and soft.

His hands contracted around her for an instant before he eased her back into her seat and took a deep breath, gripping the steering wheel hard. He lifted his head, glancing behind them at an approaching car.

He took another breath and put the car in gear, easing across the intersection and then speeding up again, changing gears with smooth ease. He pulled a cigarette from his pocket and handed it to her.

"How about lighting that for me?" he asked quietly.

"May I . . . have one, too?"

He handed her another one, with a curious glance. "Do you smoke?"

"No," she confessed. "I just need something."

"Am I that potent?" he murmured with a forced laugh.

"Don't joke about it, please," she murmured as she lit his cigarette and handed it to him, turning back to light her own.

"I have to," he said. "Physical attraction is a damned poor basis for a relationship. I don't want involvement. I've had all I can stand of it for one lifetime."

She sat back against the seat, tempted to deny what she was feeling. But she couldn't. Having it out in the open was the best way to cope with it, after all.

"And you're not the type for an affair," he added curtly, his eyes pinning hers for an instant. "There's no way I'm going to take a virgin into my bed just to satisfy a temporary hunger."

She dropped her eyes to the heavy rise and fall of his chest. Where the shirt was open, thick black hair showed, and she remembered desperately wanting to open his shirt and touch him there the night before. She hadn't, though, and probably it was just as well. Her eyes turned away from his sensuous masculinity.

"Thank you for that," she said quietly. She took a careful draw from the cigarette and blew out a cloud of smoke without inhaling. "I feel very vulnerable with you. I didn't expect it to be like that...."

"Neither did I," he said. He turned onto another country road and they passed through miles of open country with only an occasional house or service station or country store. He laughed shortly. "You were a new experience for me. I can't remember a woman ever crying when I made love to her."

She stared out at the passing landscape, the cigarette hanging forgotten between her fingers. "You're very experienced," she murmured.

"And you're very inexperienced. My God, it was sweet," he said half under his breath, glancing toward her. "Something I'll remember all my life."

Her eyes lifted to his and moved quickly away. "So will I," she confessed.

He drew in a slow breath and stared straight ahead at the road. "I'm so damned noble," he muttered. "All I need is a white horse and a halo."

She managed a smile. "Or a unicorn," she suggested.

"They were rumored to be fond of virgins, weren't they?" he asked, smiling back. "Why aren't you one of those modern women who take the pill and notch their bedposts? It would make my life so much easier right now."

Mine, too, she thought, but she wouldn't admit it. He didn't want an answer anyway, so she said nothing.

"Come on, talk," he said after a minute, his cigarette sending up curls of smoke. "Are you afraid of sex?"

She curled up in her seat as far as the shoulder harness would allow and shrugged. "I don't know. I don't think so. I just don't like temporary things. I want a home and children . . ." She glanced at him apprehensively.

"Don't pull your punches," he said quietly, meeting her apologetic gaze. "I did my grieving when it happened. It still hurts, but not as much, and I'm not that sensitive about chance remarks. Except," he added with a rueful smile, "deliberately cutting ones. As you found out."

"I understand now why it hurts to talk about her," she said gently. "I won't ever ask again."

He crushed out the cigarette and laid his hand on the console, palm up. "Give me your hand."

Without thinking, she laid her free one in that warm, callused grasp, and felt his fingers close snugly around hers. Tingles of pleasure worked their way through her body, and involuntarily, she increased the pressure.

"I'll tell you all about Jessica one day," he said quietly. "We'll get together one New Year's Eve and share a bottle of Irish whiskey and cry on each other's shoulders."

"I can just picture that," she murmured drily. "You, crying on anybody's shoulder."

"Being a man doesn't make me superhuman, honey," he reminded her. "I did my share of crying after the crash. I'm not ashamed of it, either."

"I didn't think you would be. It takes a strong man to cry," she said. Her fingers tangled in his.

"We can't be lovers," he said quietly.

"No," she agreed in a whisper.

His fingers contracted. "Then be my friend, Kenna."

She smiled, feeling a sudden urge to burst into tears, because she wanted more than that lukewarm arrangement. But if it was all that was available, it would have to do. After all, she wanted Denny... didn't she?

"How about your sister-in-law?" she teased.

His face hardened, darkened. He let her hand go.

"That reminds me, we'd better come up with some plans for next weekend."

"Why?"

"Because Margo's going to be in Argentina for the next two weeks, and Dad's having an anniversary party for my stepmother. You're sure to be invited, and I don't want Denny having it too easy." He glanced at her with a cool smile. "He likes competing with me, you see. Anything I want, he wants."

"Is that why he took up law?" she asked.

He nodded. "He's very competitive. I've got a long jump on him. That rankles. Especially now, when Dad's thinking of retiring from the computer corporation he owns."

She studied his broad face. "He'll expect one of you to take it over, won't he?" she asked, suddenly understanding.

He nodded and turned onto the highway that led to his parents' home.

"Would you like that?" she asked.

He frowned thoughtfully. "I don't know. I like what I do. I'm not sure I could make the transition from attorney to businessman. Or that I'd want to."

"But Denny would." She was sounding him out.

He glanced at her. "Yes, he would."

"Then, where's the problem?"

"My father is the problem. He doesn't think Denny's mature enough to assume that much responsibility.

"Denny's very capable at law," she remarked.

His eyes darkened. "Yes," he agreed curtly. "But corporate administration is a far cry from running a one-man law office."

He was right, much as she hated admitting it. It was hard enough for Denny to say no to potential clients. And, unlike Regan, he didn't practice criminal law, confining himself instead to divorces and property settlements and business law. He didn't have the killer instinct. But Regan did. He could hire and fire and assume responsibility for his mistakes, if there were any, without looking for scapegoats. He was strong enough to take criticism, and that was what the job called for. She could see very well why Mr. Cole would want his eldest to take over his corporation when he stepped down.

"What are you thinking about?" he asked finally.

"How you'd look in a tutu with a magic wand," she murmured wickedly.

He glared at her. "Wait until I stop this car, and then say that again."

"Do I look stupid?" She sighed, unable to take her eyes from him. "For a fairly ugly man, you're not bad."

He burst out laughing. "Does that mean you're ready to take back your apology for calling me a beast?"

"No," she told him. "If you remember, that particular beast changed into a handsome prince."

"He didn't have a nose that was broken in two places and big feet," he reminded her.

"Stop making fun of my friend," she chided gently.

He smiled at that, and reached out to ruffle her hair as he pulled the car into the long, paved driveway that led up to the two-story brick home where his parents lived on Lake Lanier.

Kenna had been there many times for business meetings and had always loved the house. It was gray brick, built on the order of an English Tudor home, but with unique variations, like the Victorian turret at one end, and the stained-glass skylight above the front door. All around it were trimmed boxwood, azaleas, camellias, and dogwood trees, along with a glorious profusion of blooming bulbs. A white latticework gazebo stood in the middle of the rose garden.

"I don't think I'll ever see another place on earth as beautiful as this," she remarked.

"It was my grandfather's home," he said. "He had it built to his own specifications. The gardens were my mother's idea," he added. "And Dad's kept them just as they were when I was a boy."

"How old were you when you lost your mother?" she asked.

"Eight," he said. He smiled. "I gave my stepmother hell for two years. After that, she began to grow on me."

"I know exactly what you mean," she murmured. Over the years Kenna had become very fond of Abbie Cole.

He parked the car in the big garage behind the house, and opened her door for her. When she was outside, he pulled her against him and walked her toward the house with his big arm around her shoulders.

"For appearances," he reminded her with a grin. "You're not supposed to enjoy it."

Her own arm snaked around his waist. "Heaven forbid that I should enjoy it," she said demurely, flirting with her eyes.

"Watch yourself," he muttered, pinching her arm and making her jump. "I've always wondered how it would feel to make love to a woman on the floor of the gazebo...."

"I'll behave," she promised him, "with utmost decorum. I won't even try to rip open your shirt."

"You'd better not," he warned as they started toward the back door, which was just opening. "My chest is an erogenous zone. And

I know just where yours is, too, baby," he added outrageously.

Before she had time to gasp, blush, or snap at him, his tall, gray-headed father was striding toward them, wearing a dark gray business suit and carrying a briefcase. Behind him was his small, very pretty wife, her platinum hair curling softly around her delicate face. She was smiling as usual.

"Hello and goodbye," Angus Cole said, shaking his son's hand and grinning at Kenna. "I'm off to Seattle for a conference. Don't eat up all my cheese crackers and keep your hands off my Napoleon brandy," he added with a scowl in Regan's direction. "Watch him, Abbie," he called to his wife.

"Yes, darling," the older woman promised. "I'll only let him drink your thirty-year-old Scotch, is that all right?"

Angus muttered something as he climbed into his black Mercedes and roared off, tooting the horn abrasively.

"Hello, dear," Mrs. Cole laughed, hugging Regan. "Hi, Kenna, welcome back, where have you been for the past two months, and what in the world have you done to yourself, you're gorgeous!" she said all in one breath.

"I've been busy," Kenna managed, as she hugged the shorter woman back. "How are you? You look gorgeous yourself."

"In jeans and a sweatshirt?" she laughed, indicating her clothes. "I've been digging in the rose garden."

"I told you about that buried treasure," Regan said drily. "The pirates buried it on the coast, not here."

"Spoilsport," his stepmother grumbled darkly. "Anyway, I'm digging up worms, not gold. A good worm is the best fertilizer God ever made. I'm transplanting them from your father's fish-bait bed into my petunias."

"God help you if he catches you," Regan replied.

"Tell him," Mrs. Cole challenged, "and I'll tell him what really happened to the Mercedes the night you took that Olson girl to the senior prom."

He sighed. "I'll keep your dark secret if you'll keep mine, Abbie," he promised.

"Fair enough. Denny and Margo are down by the lake feeding the swans," she said. "Want to come in and have coffee?"

Regan shook his head. "We'll bring them back with us and have it then."

Abbie Cole was watching the two of them with sharp, interested eyes. She smiled. "Is there something in the air?"

"Spring," Regan told her.

"Is that so? Well, mind the dog, he's loose out there somewhere," she added, waving them off.

"Pooch?" Kenna asked, scanning the landscape for the familiar toy collie.

"Pooch. And he'll be one long furry clump of mud and leaves, as usual." He glanced at her. "I'll shave his fur if he gets one speck of mud on that dress. It suits you."

She beamed. "Thank you, fairy godfather," she murmured.

"Stop that. Uh-oh, watch out!"

The warning almost came too late. Pooch came flying up from the vicinity of the lake, his fur as sleek as a seal's from swimming and as muddy as a rain-swollen river. He headed straight for Kenna, who always played with him despite his antisocial tendencies.

She was looking for a tree to climb when Regan swooped and lifted her like a child in his big arms. "Down, Pooch," he said in his courtroom voice, and the dog immediately sat down and whined at him, looking so impish he might have been a furry human.

"You do that very well," Kenna remarked, reveling in the pleasure of being held so close to him, in the sheer male strength of the big body supporting hers.

"I practice on hostile witnesses," he informed her. His eyes searched hers.

"You're so strong," she murmured, letting her hands rest around his shoulders. Her voice sounded girlish, and she flushed at the inane remark.

"Sorry," she added demurely, "I didn't mean to sound star-struck. Of course you're strong, you're as big as a tree."

"Not quite." He swung her around, laughing at the way she clung to him, her face flushed and radiant, her eyes laughing back.

He buried his face in her soft hair and deliberately crushed her close. "You smell delicious, woman," he growled in her ear. "I'd like to take several bites of you."

"You'd poison yourself," she assured him.

"That's not likely, or I'd have died last night." He lifted his head and looked into her wide, misty eyes. "Why did you cry while I was loving you?" he whispered.

Shudders of wild pleasure rippled through her at his wording, and her lips parted on a trembling breath. "Because it was so beautiful," she managed unsteadily.

His eyes dropped to her parted lips. "We'd burn each other alive if we made love completely," he said, and his deep voice sounded as unsteady as her own. There was a tremor in the arms that held her. He moved, brushing her lips with his own, creating a shiver of sensation that made her gasp. "All I have to do is touch you," he said, repeating the motion again and again, until her mouth followed his, pleading for more. "All I have to do is touch you, and I start aching like a boy of fifteen. I want you, Kenna, I want to lay you down in the grass and open that dress and bare your body to the sun and my eyes and my mouth . . . !"

Even as he spoke he was pressing her lips apart with his, so that she could feel every warm, smoky curve of his mouth meeting hers exactly. He opened her mouth with a whispering pressure, his tongue teasing, his lips brushing, cherishing in a perfect orgy of foreplay that made her moan and clutch at his broad shoulders.

"Kiss me," she ground out, aching for it, for completion, perfection. "Kiss me, kiss me hard, and don't stop, don't ever stop!" she moaned against his seeking mouth.

She trembled at the sudden rough crush of it, grinding her mouth into his, loving the intimacy of it, the feel of his tongue, the taste.

He groaned something she couldn't hear, and his big arm tightened, dragging her breasts against the fabric that separated them from his hard chest.

Only Pooch's sudden fierce bark kept the kiss from going much further than its wild beginning. Regan drew back from her mouth with eyes blacker than midnight, his body trembling as he held her. He dragged his eyes away from the sight of her hungry, soft eyes and looked over her body at Denny and Margo.

"We've got company," he said tautly. He set her back on her feet, and drew in a long, shuddering breath. "We've got to stop this," he reminded her.

She searched his face with quick, possessive eyes and wondered at her wild reaction to him. "Yes," she agreed.

He wasn't even trying to look away. "You trembled," he breathed.

"So did you."

He dragged a hand through his hair and glowered down at her. "I am not taking you to bed," he ground out.

"Wait until you're asked," she flashed back, her eyes sparkling, her face radiant, so that she held his appreciative gaze against his will.

"The point behind teaching you to be seductive was not to teach you how to seduce me," he said shortly. "I am not going to get sexually involved with a virgin."

"So you keep saying," she returned. "Then why don't you stop kissing me and saying outrageously suggestive things to me?"

"Why don't you stop begging to be kissed?" he fired at her.

"Can I help it if God gave you unbelievable talents in lovemaking to compensate for your lack of looks?" she asked.

He scowled. "Kenna . . ."

"All right, all right," she sighed. "If that's how you appreciate my quite understandable weakness, then just don't expect me to take my dress off for you, so there."

He was fighting a chuckle. He lost. "Damn you, stop flirting with me."

"Me, flirting?" she asked, her eyebrows going straight up in mock innocence. "I wouldn't dream of it. You men are all alike, flaunting your gorgeous bodies at us poor women and then getting all insulted when we try to show our appreciation of them."

He burst out laughing. "I've created a monster," he observed, glancing toward Margo and Denny, who were coming along the path toward them. "Whatever happened to that blushing little virgin who used to hide in the records room to avoid me?"

"You'll have to ask my fairy godfather," she told him. "I haven't the foggiest idea where the poor frumpy thing went."

"I called you that, didn't I?" he murmured, watching her with quiet, dark eyes. "I think I even meant it, at the time." He sighed. "What a transformation."

"I'm glad you appreciate your own handiwork. I hope Denny does," she added, just to spite him, and turned a beaming smile toward his stepbrother.

Margo was glaring at her, but she pretended not to notice. "Hi, Denny, Regan brought me down for the day."

"How nice," Denny said, and he seemed to mean it. He stepped forward, and bent to brush his mouth over Kenna's cheek. She felt a pleasant tingle, but nothing like the electric charge she felt in Regan's presence. Two years of patient waiting had been rewarded, but too late. Now Denny seemed strangely unthreatening. Pleasant, fun to be around, very nice. But not stormy and physically dangerous like Regan. She stared at the shorter man and all at once knew why she felt that way.

Regan was handing her Denny on a silver platter. And quite suddenly she knew that she didn't want Denny, because she was hopelessly in love with Regan. Regan, who didn't want involvement, who was going to be her friend from now on, because he only desired her. But he didn't seduce virgins and he was through with love. The irony of it almost made her cry.

"We are glad that you were free to join us," Margo said with cold courtesy, clinging to Denny's arm with the tenacity of flypaper.

"We thought we'd sprawl under the trees and watch the lake for a while," Regan said, moving close to Kenna. He caught her hand in his and smiled down at her with every part of his face except his eyes. "I'd planned to spend some time with Dad, but we passed him on his way out, and Abbie's hunting worms with a spade. On the Sabbath too."

Margo looked puzzled, but Denny laughed and squeezed her hand. She was wearing a red silk blouse with white slacks and shoes, and against her dark coloring, the combination was devastating. Even in her new finery, Kenna felt dowdy by comparison and envied Margo her perfect sight. Glasses were the pits.

She pushed the frames up over her hair with a flourish. "I love your blouse," she told Margo. "I wish I could wear red, but I look washed out in it."

Margo started, as if the compliment were unexpected. "Oh," she murmured. "Thank you."

"We could go and sit with you, but Margo has to catch a plane at eight," Denny said apologetically, and his eyes kept going back to Kenna and her wispy, sexy dress. "I have to drive her to the airport."

"Going home for a visit?" Regan asked politely.

Margo smiled. "A necessary one," she agreed. "Some European breeders are coming to see our bloodstock. Papa insists that I help him decide which of the Thoroughbreds to sell. It will be a difficult choice," she sighed. "I love them every one."

"Thoroughbreds?" Regan murmured, glancing toward Denny with a frown.

"Margo's family breeds champion racing horses," the younger man replied. "Among their other interests. They also own several hundred thousand acres of land, herds of cattle, international real estate . . ."

"Please, you embarrass me," Margo said quickly, touching Denny's arm. "It is not proper to speak of such things. It is like, how you say, blowing one's pipe?"

"Horn," Denny corrected. He threw an arm around Margo. "Care to have coffee with us before we leave?" he asked his stepbrother. "The lake will still be there later."

"I think we would," Regan replied. "Honey?" he added, glancing down at Kenna.

"I'm pretty thirsty," she confided.

He nodded, tugging at her hand. "Then let's sit down and rescue the worms from Abbie."

Kenna walked quietly at his side, puzzling over Margo's confession. So the foreign woman wasn't a mercenary poverty case. She wondered how that tidbit of information was going to affect Regan's point of view. Not that it mattered to her anymore. She was in enough mental turmoil as it was.

They spent an hour inside, drinking coffee and talking. Regan was obviously impressed by Margo's intelligence, and the South American woman warmed to his interest. She even managed a kind word for Kenna, although she kept darting concerned glances in Denny's direction. The younger man's fascination with Kenna was becoming more obvious by the minute. Great, Kenna thought miserably, staring down into her coffee. She'd spent two years mooning over Denny, and *now* he was interested, when it was too late, when her heart had been taken over by a man she had thought she hated, and there was no hope of her ever getting it back whole.

"I like your new look, Kenna," Denny told her while Margo was saying her good-byes to Abbie in the kitchen. "So different..."

She avoided his eyes and tried not to look at Regan, because she didn't want to see the contempt in his face. "I had help," she murmured with a smile.

"Yes, I know," Denny said curtly, glancing toward Regan, who was idly thumbing through a book over by the bookcase. "Are you getting involved with him?" he asked, moving closer and lowering his voice.

Kenna looked startled. "What do you mean?"

"I mean," he said shortly, glancing apprehensively at Regan, "there's no future in it."

"Isn't there?" Kenna asked. "Why?"

"Because he was married once," he said flatly, meeting her level gaze. "She died, and he's never gotten over it. I should have told you that before . . ."

"Regan told me," she interrupted. "Everything."

He blinked. "He doesn't talk about it to anyone, he never has," he said on a frown.

"I'm not just anyone, Denny," she said with a smug grin.

He sighed angrily and rammed his hands in his pockets. "How about having lunch with me tomorrow? I need to talk to you."

"All right, boss," she agreed.

"Don't call me that," he said uncomfortably. He glanced past her and saw Margo and Abbie coming out of the kitchen. "We'll talk later. Watch yourself."

"Oh, I let other people do that," Kenna said demurely, avoiding his gaze. She smiled at Margo. "I hope you have a good trip," she said.

Margo glanced uncomfortably from Kenna to Denny and frowned. "I'm sure I shall," she said. "However, it will only be for a week."

"I thought you said two weeks," Denny remarked.

Margo smiled sweetly. "Perhaps you didn't listen, darling," she said, her dark eyes flashing.

Denny scowled. "Perhaps you didn't tell me you'd changed your mind ... darling," he returned.

"I think we should go," Margo said curtly. "Thank you for your hospitality, Mrs. Cole. I hope to spend more time with you when I return. Regan, Miss Dean," she added, nodding at each in turn. She glanced toward Denny and swept out the door.

"See you tomorrow," Denny told Kenna and Regan. "Bye, Mom," he added, pausing to hug his mother. "See you. Thanks for the coffee."

"Any time, son," Abbie murmured absently, watching him hurry out the door with a frown. "Now, what's going on?" she grumbled, glaring toward Regan.

He arched both eyebrows innocently. "How should I know?"

"You know everything," Abbie returned. "Especially where Denny's concerned. Spill it, Regan, what's going on? Is it something to do with you and Kenna? Is he jealous? Is he going to marry Miss de la Vera?"

"No, I don't know, yes, probably, your guess is as good as mine," Regan rattled off, catching Kenna's arm. "That answers your barrage of questions, Abbie, and you can spend the rest of the afternoon fitting it all together. Kenna and I have to go. Thanks for the coffee. *Ciao.*"

Kenna barely had time to call good-bye and add her thanks to his before he dragged her out the door and shoved her into the car.

"Do you mind?" she gasped, rubbing her arm.

"Sorry, honey, but if we'd stayed a minute longer, the Spanish Inquisition would have been in session," he grinned, starting the Porsche. "You know Abbie by now, don't you? She smells a scoop."

"That's right, she met your father when she was working as a newspaperwoman, didn't she?" She grinned. "I'd forgotten."

"She never does. And she could pry information out of a clam with a plastic dipstick." He pulled out of the driveway, tooting his horn just as his father had, in the old family tradition. "What was Denny whispering in your ear?"

"He's taking me to lunch tomorrow to warn me off you," she said with a wicked grin. "He's afraid you're going to corrupt me and lead me into a life of sin."

"I'd love to," he said, with a wistful glance in her direction. "Your place or mine?"

"You just got through saying that you don't seduce virgins," she said.

"Damn," he grumbled. "I forgot."

"I'll keep reminding you, so that you don't have lapses," she promised.

He laughed softly as he lit a cigarette and smoked it quietly. "Where do you want to go?"

"I like riding around," she confessed, settling comfortably in her seat.

"So do I. We'll ride, then." He turned on the radio. "Classical, soft rock, hard rock, easy listening?" he asked.

"Soft rock," she said immediately.

He pushed one of the preset buttons and laughed at her expression. "I'm only thirty-five," he reminded her.

She blinked. She hadn't really thought of him in terms of age until now, but come to think of it, he didn't look old. Mature, yes, masculine, yes, but not old.

"Ten years older than me," she murmured.

"And Denny," he added, smiling. "Though he gets mistaken for twenty-two."

"Why did you want to be a lawyer?" she asked, curious.

"I don't know," he said honestly. "I suppose it had something to do with a library full of Perry Mason novels. I like details, I like finding hidden things." He shrugged his broad shoulders. "I like the challenge, I suppose."

"Why criminal law?" she persisted.

"Because it's the most challenging field," he said immediately. "Life and death."

"Yes, it's that," she agreed, recalling cases she'd typed for him, transcripts she'd copied, all the bits and pieces of information that filled a plea, and that might save a man's life or keep him out of prison.

He glanced at her. "Why did you want to be a legal secretary?"

"I needed a job, and I was tired of working for a bank," she replied with a smile. "Numbers aren't really my forte. But I liked law, and Denny had a one-girl office where I'd mostly be my own boss."

"And then he took in a partner..." he murmured drily.

"You were horrible to me!" she said, glaring toward him. "Absolutely horrible. I don't know how I managed to get through those months without writing out my resignation on your desk top in red lipstick."

"I hoped you would," he said quietly. "You bothered me. Frumpy outfits and all, you really got to me."

"Denny said the secretary you had in New York was a real dish," she murmured, glancing sideways.

"She was. And if she'd stood in the middle of the floor naked, I'd have walked past her on my way to court without blinking an eye." He crushed out the cigarette. "I've been more involved with work than women since Jessica died."

None of it was making sense, and she stared at him pointedly, trying to make the pieces fit.

"You have a delicious young body," he said matter-of-factly. "And I didn't need a program to tell that it hadn't been out on loan to anyone who asked." He sighed deeply as they wound down a picturesque country road, his eyes dark and curious as they swept toward her and away again. "I was curious about you, about why you deliberately downplayed your looks."

"You were just plain hostile," she corrected. "I felt the same way about you, and I wasn't curious about your looks, either."

He chuckled softly. "What looks?"

"There was an actor when I was a kid, who played in a Western TV series," she told him. "He was uglier than sin, but he had a way with women that made him the hottest property going." She smiled in his direction. "Of course, he didn't have big feet."

"My curse," he admitted. "I was always falling over them when I was a boy."

"Now other people fall over them," she murmured, and reminded him about the client who tripped over Regan's large feet and fell headfirst into a potted palm.

He laughed with her. "I thought the leaves suited him, at the time." The smile faded as the music began to change to a slow, sensuous tune that set a new mood. He glanced at her. "Denny's interested."

"Yes, I know," she said.

"Margo knows too. She doesn't like it."

"And you thought she was mercenary," she murmured.

"Nobody's perfect. An heiress, no less. A very possessive heiress, and unless I miss my guess, she's going to try to add my stepbrother to her acquisitions."

"Would you really mind, knowing what you do about her?" she asked curiously.

He didn't answer that. His fingers went to his pocket, produced another cigarette and lit it. "Don't jump at anything Denny offers, will you?" he asked quietly. "You'll throw the game if you give in too soon."

"God forbid," she said. She leaned back in the seat and glanced at his set features. "How soon is too soon?"

"Let him sweat for a week," he suggested.

"Margo will be back in a week."

He took a long draw from the cigarette. "So she will." He turned up the radio. "Do what you please, Kenna. I've set the scene. The rest is up to you." His jaw was set and he looked grim. "You could do worse than Denny, if he's what you really want."

Her eyes narrowed as they studied his profile and she felt a cold, dull emptiness inside. He'd already said that he had nothing to offer her except an affair. And she wasn't stupid enough to think she could survive one with him. She wouldn't be able to let go. Never having was better than letting go, she supposed. It looked as if it would have to be.

He'd admitted being interested in her physically, but why had that made him so hostile? And what had he meant about being more involved with work than women—that he didn't have affairs? And was that why he was antagonistic toward Kenna? Her mind felt as if it were on a merry-go-round trying to find answers.

She turned her face toward the window, feeling lost. She'd felt so close to him. She'd learned things about him, she'd begun to like him, genuinely like him. Now it was all over, and he'd done his improvement bit, and he was going on to bigger and better things. And Kenna was to go after Denny and take him away from Margo and live happily ever after. The end. Except that this wasn't the right fairy tale, either.

She closed her eyes and let herself drift with the music. The laughing camaraderie they'd shared earlier seemed to have died completely, leaving a grudging truce in its place. The taciturn man at her side looked like a man who'd never smiled in his life. And what frightened her was that he might be setting a pattern for the future. At least be my friend, she pleaded silently. Be my friend, Regan, don't walk out of my life. Before they reached the city, tears were threatening behind her closed eyelids.

Chapter Seven

The office felt different when Kenna walked in the next morning. She was wearing the tailored navy suit Regan had bought for her with a white V-necked blouse and a navy and white scarf to set it off. She looked jaunty and young and on top of the world, despite her sleepless night.

Denny was pacing the floor when she walked in. He turned and stared at her, running his eyes up and down her slender body.

"I just can't get over the change," he remarked as she walked slowly, gracefully, to hang up her coat, using all the tricks Regan had gone to such pains to teach her.

She smiled at him. "You'll get used to it," she assured him. Her eyes went to the closed door of Regan's office, and her heart jumped at the thought of seeing him this morning.

"He's gone," Denny said flatly, watching her curious gaze.

"Gone?" she echoed. Her eyes widened, and she felt cold all of a sudden.

"To New York for the week," he informed her with a smile. "One of those spur of the moment decisions he makes. No warning, no nothing, I found a note on my desk."

She searched his eyes. "Did he leave one for me?" she asked.

He shook his head. "Nope, I figured he'd already told you. How odd that he didn't."

She avoided his suspicious appraisal and sat down at her desk. "Did Margo get off all right?"

"Margo?" He grimaced. "Yes," he said darkly, "she took off in a cloud of smoke."

She lifted her eyes, surprised at the venom in his tone. Denny was never sarcastic. "That sounds strange."

He looked down at her broodingly, his arms folded over his chest, his blond hair gleaming in the sunlight that streamed through the open curtains. "We had a knock-down, drag-out fight, if you want to know," he told her. "Over you."

Her eyes widened. "Me?"

"She thought I was paying you too much attention." He smiled at her, a new kind of smile, teasing and flirtatious and interested. "And I suppose she was right."

Her eyebrows arched. She lifted her eyes to his and lowered them quickly. "I'm flattered," she replied. That was all she was, unfortunately, not thrilled half to death as she would have been a month, even a week, ago.

"I'd never have known you were the same woman," he continued. "Everything about you has changed all of a sudden. Regan's influence?"

She smiled. "He has a way with him," she murmured demurely.

His face clouded. "Yes, I know. And a way with women, period," he added coldly. "I could never keep track of them until he married Jessica. He draws them like honey."

That hurt. She wondered if he meant it to, or realized how successful the remark was. Now she'd spend the whole week thinking about Regan with other women in New York, and she'd never sleep a wink tonight.

"He's rich," she remarked.

"Yes, he's that," he agreed. "And macho. Regan's always had everything he wanted."

She read the hurt in that cold statement, and she felt a surge of compassion for him. "Growing up in his shadow wasn't easy, was it?" she asked.

He laughed shortly. "That's an understatement. No matter what I ever did, Regan did it better. His grades were higher, his athletic prowess put me in the shade, he could make Dad sit up and take notice if he made a suggestion about the corporation...." He shrugged. "I'm jealous of him, you know. Men like Regan make up their own rules as they go along. He's one of a kind."

She agreed with that in her heart. He was one of a kind, and she didn't think she'd ever stop wanting him. But Regan had nothing to offer her.

She glanced up at him. "Does that lunch invitation still stand?"

"Of course." He grinned. "I'll take you to Tonie's for spaghetti."

"I love spaghetti," she sighed.

"I know, that's why I suggested it. I hate to mention mundane subjects, but how about getting the mail and let's answer it? I've got a case at ten."

"Sure thing, counselor," she murmured sweetly, and got up to go get it. His eyes followed her all the way out the door.

The morning went by quickly, especially with Denny and Regan both out and the phones ringing constantly. Kenna finally got a minute to put Regan's mail on his desk, and she found herself standing by it for a long time, just staring at the huge swivel chair that barely contained his massive bulk. She missed him. The color had gone out of the world for her, and she wondered absently if this was going to set the pace for the rest of her life? Surely she could forget him. After all, what she'd felt for Denny had already begun to fade quietly away to leave affection in its place. Perhaps it would be that way when she finally got over Regan. When she was 106 years old or so.

Denny was back right at noon, and she rode down to Tonie's with him in his blue Mercedes.

The restaurant was crowded, but they were seated in a tiny alcove, where they ate spaghetti and garlic bread and drank a pot of coffee between them.

Denny talked about the office and his father's corporation. And it seemed that Regan wasn't the only one worrying about what would happen when Angus retired.

"Regan would never be satisfied running the corporation," Denny said. "He likes what he does too much. On the other hand," he added with a bitter laugh, "Dad doesn't think I could handle it."

"Have you ever considered asking him to let you into the administration for a while, on probation?" she asked. She smiled at him impishly. "And show him what you can do?"

He brightened. "What a thought. No, I hadn't." He pursed his lips. "It would mean giving up the practice, of course, and Regan would probably go back to New York and take up his own again. I've always had the feeling he threw in with me to give me a head start, anyway."

Kenna could have bitten her tongue out. Now she'd just put her job in jeopardy. If Regan went back to New York, she surely wouldn't be asked to go with him, and it would be the end of seeing him every day.

"You're white as a sheet," Denny observed, frowning. "What is it, are you sick?"

She swallowed down a sip of hot coffee. "Just indigestion," she countered. "That sauce was spicy!"

"I know what you mean." He studied her. "Of course, you're upset," he said quickly. "I didn't mean to imply that you wouldn't have a job, Kenna. You could always come to the corporation with me." He grinned boyishly. "You'd love it; it's full of potted plants and light. You're always complaining that my office looks dark and dead."

She managed a wan smile for him and tugged at her scarf with restless fingers. "I suppose I could," she murmured, hurting as she thought of Regan moving out of her life forever. Even though it might be the best thing that could happen, the thought brought a pain like nothing she'd ever felt.

"How involved have you gotten with my stepbrother?" he asked gently, and looked genuinely concerned.

Her eyes lifted. "Well . . ."

"Don't let him cut you up," he said softly. "He's a sausage grinder. Nothing and no one means a damned thing to him since Jessica was killed. He only goes through the motions of living.'' He set his cup down. ''They had to drag him away from the graveyard,'' he added, remembering. ''I've never seen anything like it. I didn't know people could grieve that much . . .'' He put down his napkin, unaware of the pain in Kenna's eyes. ''We'd better get back. Want to stroll through the park on the way? I think there's some kind of folk concert going on.''

''I'd like that,'' she agreed. Anything to get her mind off Regan. She smiled at him. ''I'd really like that.''

They wandered hand in hand through the wooded park, where a group of folk musicians were playing to an audience of young people seated on the grass. It was a balmy spring day, and Kenna was holding Denny's hand and should have been on top of the world. But her mind was on that big, dark, lonely man who'd lived so long with his grief that he'd forgotten how bright and beautiful the world could be. She wanted to soothe the lines of pain in his face and give him peace. She wanted to sit and listen to him and love him all her life.

Tears misted her eyes and she bit her lip to stifle them. She missed him so. And he was probably out consoling himself with some woman, she thought suddenly with a flare of violent, unreasonable jealousy. She could picture him with a blonde, someone who'd remind him of his beautiful Jessica—his dark skin and curling body hair pressing down on smooth, pink flesh.

She gasped, and Denny stopped to stare at her. "What's wrong?" he asked.

"Nothing," she said quickly. "Let's go closer."

They stood just outside the circle of spectators and listened to a bluesy folk song about lost love, while Kenna tried her best to forget the embarrassing picture that had painted itself boldly behind her eyes. Why should she care what Regan was doing? He had told her that he wasn't going to involve himself with anyone ever again, except physically, so why should she care if he did it with some other woman? Some sophisticated woman on the pill who wouldn't complicate his life by getting pregnant or clinging to him. Tears burned her eyes. He had to numb the ache, of course, from time to time. She shouldn't begrudge him what little peace he could find. But she did, she did, and she wanted him!

Denny clasped her hand, and grinned down at her. She smiled back. This was nice. Pleasant. Just a friendly kind of camaraderie that would have put her on top of a cloud once. Now all it did was remind her of what she could never have. Regan had spoiled her for any other man.

They finished their work for the day and Denny took her home. She invited him in and cooked supper for him. As the week went on they spent a lot of time together, and Thursday night after he'd taken her to see a science-fiction movie, he kissed her at her front door.

It wasn't bad. Very nice, in fact. But his lips were cool and gentlemanly and very tender. Nothing as fierce and demanding as Regan's. The insistent intimacy of his kisses could make her blush even in memory. Denny was nothing like his stepbrother.

He moved back, smiling at her strange expression, because he thought he was responsible for it.

"You shouldn't do that," she said softly. "Margo..."

His brows drew together. "What would Margo care?" he asked harshly. "She's off in Argentina with that ever-so-suave neighbor of hers, probably having a ball every night. So what would it matter to her if I kissed you?"

So that was it. They'd had a fight and Margo had taunted him with another man, and he was jealous and hurt and wanted to get even. She almost smiled, but caught herself in time to spare his pride. Let him think he was succeeding in catching his secretary's eye; let him salve his ego. Thank goodness she was over her crush on him, or it would have cut her to ribbons, being used as he was unintentionally using her.

"Suave neighbor, huh?" she murmured, peeking up at him through her lashes.

He shrugged. "Some guy she's known since she was a kid."

"Oh, those are dangerous, all right. But she's supposed to be back tomorrow, isn't she?" she added.

He seemed to brighten. "Supposed to," he agreed. "Well, I'll say good night. See you in the morning."

She smiled. "Of course."

He started down the hall and looked back over his shoulder. "Heard from Regan?"

Her own eyes clouded. "No," she said gently, turning back into her apartment. "Good night."

She hadn't heard from Regan for the whole week, nor had she expected to. Apparently he'd decided to give Denny a clear field and let her do what she pleased. That hurt, too, that he didn't care enough to fight for her. But why should he, when he didn't want her, except briefly and physically?

"Do you want to ride up to Gainesville with Margo and me in the morning?" Denny asked on Friday afternoon, just before Margo was due to return. Now he seemed to feel guilty that he'd been courting Kenna, and didn't know what to do about it.

"No," she told him. "I'll wait for Regan. I'm sure he'll be back in time for the anniversary get-together."

"He promised Dad he would," he agreed, "and Regan never breaks promises. Don't forget to pack an overnight bag, Mom's got a room ready for you. The four of us will find something to do." He looked hunted. "Kenna, about this week . . ."

She touched his arm lightly. "It's been great fun. But only fun," she said. "I know you've missed Margo. I was glad to fill in for her."

He flushed wildly and averted his eyes to her desk. "God, I'm sorry," he ground out. "I didn't realize until this morning that you might have gotten the wrong idea."

"I didn't," she assured him with a genuine smile. "I know how it feels to miss someone until you ache."

His eyes came up to probe hers. "Regan," he said.

She covered up her typewriter. "Time to go home, counselor. Margo will be waiting."

"Kenna, don't let him hurt you," he said suddenly.

She laughed bitterly. "Now you tell me," she sighed.

His hands gestured helplessly. "You're such a babe in the woods, and he's an old fox. I don't know how to put this..."

"He doesn't prey on lambs," she told him gently. "He told me so himself, and he's stuck to it. The problems are all on my side, not his. He's been perfectly honest. We're...friends," she said, almost choking on the word. "Because that's all he has to offer, and he won't take any more than that. And yes, I've offered," she said harshly. Tears moistened her long lashes. "On my knees ... !" Her voice broke, and Denny grimaced.

"You poor kid," he said with genuine sympathy, and pulled her gently into his arms. He held her while she cried, his face in her hair, his whole posture comforting. Nothing but that, only comfort.

But to the big, dark man who opened the door and stared into the office, it looked like far more than comfort. His face contorted and he hesitated uncharacteristically before he suddenly set his lips in a thin line and slammed the door behind him.

Kenna and Denny burst apart. Her heart seemed to shake wildly as she saw Regan standing there, staring at them. She knew instinctively what he was thinking, and there was nothing she could say.

"Welcome home," Denny said brightly. "Have a good trip?"

Regan nodded. His eyes went to Kenna. "Don't let me interrupt anything. I just came in to pick up my mail."

He went into his office and slammed that door too. Denny raised his eyebrows and looked down at Kenna with a speculative smile.

"Well, well," he murmured. "Someone's in a snit."

She giggled at the wording, despite the fact that her heart was breaking. Well, he'd told her to go after Denny, hadn't he? What was he so angry about?

"Think it's safe to ask if he wants any dictation taken before I leave?" she asked, dabbing at her eyes.

"Let me get out the door before you ask him, if you don't mind," he said, glancing toward Regan's office. "My insurance has lapsed, and I don't want to get caught in the crossfire."

"Rat, deserting the sinking ship," she accused. "Go ahead, leave me here alone with the dragon."

"Regan keeps ice in the bar behind his bookcase if there are any bruises," he advised. "See you tomorrow. I hope," he added.

She stuck out her tongue at him. He left, and the office became deadly quiet.

Gathering her wits, she knocked briefly at Regan's door and opened it.

He was standing by the window, one hand in his pocket, the other holding a cigarette. The beige suit he wore made him look bigger, and she hesitated in the open doorway. He didn't seem approachable anymore.

"How was your trip?" she asked after a minute, feeling his coldness like an Arctic breeze.

"Fine, thanks."

She glared at his broad back, picturing him with dazzling women dripping diamonds and sensuality. "I'm leaving," she said shortly. "Do you need anything before I go?"

He turned, his dark eyes blazing, narrowed, as they searched over her like hands feeling for breaks. "I'd have thought you'd go with him."

"He's going to pick up Margo at the airport," she began.

He laughed shortly. "Tough luck, honey. What happened, didn't you measure up?"

So that was how it was going to be, she thought miserably. The truce was over, the friendship was dead. They were going back to earlier days and hostility. Well, if that was how he wanted it, it was fine with her!

"Wouldn't you like to know?" she asked with a cold smile. "How about writing out my paycheck, counselor, so that I can cover my bills? Denny forgot.''

"Why didn't you pick his pocket?" he asked with a mocking smile. "You were close enough."

"Yes," she agreed with a wistful smile and a sigh. "I certainly was. I can't tell you how much I appreciate all your help, Mr. Cole, it sure did the trick."

He moved closer, his face hardening. "Have you slept with him?"

Her eyes popped. "That's none of your business!"

"The hell it isn't; have you slept with him?" He took her by the shoulders and actually shook her, his face frightening. "Well?"

She swallowed. "No!" she said quickly, intimidated by the tone as well as the bruising grasp.

He let her go abruptly and moved to his desk. "Make sure he's through with Margo before you tangle up your life, will you?" he asked as he pulled out the big office checkbook.

"Is that actually concern for my welfare I hear?" she asked in a quavering tone.

"No," he returned, busy writing the check. "I don't want to have to pull Denny out of a paternity suit."

She couldn't remember ever wanting to hit anyone so much—not even Regan. Her body shook with rage, but she suppressed it. She had a feeling he'd enjoy it if she attacked him.

He handed her the check and she took it with trembling fingers, her face white as a sheet. She didn't even try to thank him; she couldn't manage it.

She turned and walked back out. It only took a minute to clear her desk and put on her sweater and get her purse out of the drawer. But she was aware of him the whole time, watching her.

When she started to leave he stepped in front of her, blocking her path.

She wouldn't look up. "Will you let me by, please?" she asked as calmly as she could.

He took a deep breath, and it sighed out like an ode to weariness. "I'm sorry."

The apology was unexpected. It surprised her into looking up, and at close range his face was startling. It had new lines, deeper lines, and it was drawn. He looked as if he hadn't slept or rested since he'd been gone. That made her even madder, because she imagined him carousing till dawn in New York.

"You look horrible," she said bluntly. "Too many late nights on the town, counselor?"

"Jealous?" he taunted.

She flushed, averting her gaze to his vest. "I don't have the right to be jealous. Our relationship is all play-acting, remember? To fool Denny. To make him jealous. To take him away from Margo so that I can marry him and live happily ever after. And what the hell does it matter to you who I sleep with?" she added in a temper, glaring up at him.

Her face was extraordinarily lovely in anger, bright as a penny, radiant, animated. He looked at her as if he were starving for the sight of her.

"I don't think this is a good time to go into why it matters," he said. "Are you coming home with me tomorrow?"

She swallowed. "Denny said I could ride down with him and Margo."

"You'll ride down with me. I'll pick you up about nine. That will give us time to take the boat out on the lake, if you like."

She nodded.

He tilted her chin up. "You look lovely today," he said.

She searched his dark eyes and smiled faintly. "I wish I could lie and say you looked the same. You should have rested instead of painting the town red."

His thumb caressed her chin idly. "I haven't had a woman since Jessica died, Kenna," he said quietly.

She felt the color leave her face. "But those women in the paper, and Denny said . . ."

"What did Denny say, that I had a line at my door?" he laughed bitterly. "Denny knows even less about my private life than you do. I don't have affairs. Not since the day I met Jessica, and not since her death. Sex for its own sake appeals to me about as much as working in the nude." He let go of her chin and moved back toward his office. "I've been trying to help find enough evidence to convict a client's wife of attempted murder. It seems that since he wouldn't agree to her terms, she decided to get rid of him without the formality of a divorce. And in a much more final manner."

"My God," she breathed. "People do the craziest things to each other."

"Yes, they do," he replied harshly. "The woman's going to face some hefty criminal charges too. My client is an old friend. He asked for help, and I couldn't refuse him. That," he added curtly, "is why I look dragged out, not because I've been sleeping around."

She drew in a slow, steady breath. "I was jealous," she admitted softly, avoiding his eyes. "I'm sorry."

She opened the door to leave, but he came up behind her and his hand covered hers on the doorknob. She didn't turn, although she could feel the length of him, warm and powerful against her back.

"I won't let it happen," he said in a strained tone. "We agreed at the beginning that we'd doll you up for Denny's benefit, and that's what we've done. I won't let it happen, Kenna, I won't...!"

She was trembling, and he felt it. She knew he felt it, because all at once he caught her arms and whirled her against him. The hold he had on her was crushing, but she didn't protest. It was all of heaven to be in his arms again, to feel the strength and warmth of them, while she drowned in the scent and sight of him.

There was a tremor in his arms as they molded her against him, and she slid her own arms under his jacket, taking pleasure in the warmth of the muscles barely concealed by his shirt and vest. Her breasts were crushed softly against him, and she loved the hard brush of his thighs on her own. She loved everything about him, every single thing.

His breath sighed out unsteadily at her throat, but he didn't kiss her, or make any effort to increase the intimacy of the embrace. He simply held her against him, and that seemed to be enough.

"No more," he said finally, relaxing his hold a little. "We've got to let the bomb defuse itself. I can't live like this."

She knew instinctively what he was talking about. Her cheek nuzzled against his chest. "Why don't you just take me to bed?" she asked quietly. "There has to be a first time...."

"Yours isn't going to be with me," he said. He let her go with a hard sigh, and his eyes were weary. "I can't offer you anything except a temporary liaison. An occasional weekend. That's not my style, and to hell with what Denny thinks."

She searched his dark eyes. "Regan, is it because of Jessica?" she asked gently. "Is that why you . . . why you don't sleep around?"

"Look who's asking that question," he remarked curtly. "Why don't you sleep around?"

She laughed at the irony of it. "I'm a woman. You can't get pregnant, you know."

"That isn't the only reason you've kept your chastity," he murmured with a knowing smile.

She grimaced. "Men are supposed to be different."

He laughed softly. "I sowed my wild oats years ago, Kenna. I know what it's all about, the mystery's all gone."

Her eyes searched his quietly. "It isn't for me," she said. "Books and reality are worlds apart."

His chest rose and fell heavily as he studied her face. "That will give you something to look forward to, when you marry," he said finally. His eyes clouded. "With Denny, perhaps."

She lifted her chin proudly. "Perhaps," she agreed coldly. "I have to go."

His fingers held her upper arms tightly for a minute, and something dangerous lingered in his eyes. "I can't take the risk again," he said enigmatically.

"Oh, be safe, by all means," she agreed. "Never walk in the rain, you might catch pneumonia. Never go on a trip, the plane might crash. Never love, she might die!"

His face contorted. "What the hell do you know about love?" he asked harshly.

Her eyes fell and she pulled away from him. "I know more than you think," she said with enormous dignity. "I know how it hurts." She turned away and walked out of the office, leaving him standing there alone.

Chapter Eight

Kenna had looked forward to a beautiful day for the Coles' anniversary party, but she woke up to a driving rain outside her apartment window. It wasn't the best possible omen and she had to force down a feeling of utter dread. There was one bright spot, and that was the thought of spending a few precious hours with Regan outside the office. If only it hadn't rained. In the speedboat they could have been alone.

She dressed in navy blue slacks and a blue and white striped blouse, carrying the sea-colored gown that Regan liked so much to put on that night for the party. She felt dreamy as she packed her small overnight bag. Perhaps Regan would dance with her, at least.

At nine the doorbell rang and she rushed to let Regan in. He lifted an eyebrow at her hurry, but there was no welcoming smile on his face. A curtain had been dropped between them.

"I'm almost ready," she said, turning away. She couldn't bear to look at him. In that open-throated wine colored shirt and gray slacks, he looked good enough to wrestle down on a couch.

"There's been a change of plan," he said.

She turned, dreading what he might say. They'd canceled the party, that was it—or Denny had eloped—or...

"We're still going," he said, anticipating her nervous outburst. "But Denny and I have to fly up to Greenville about one o'clock for a quick meeting with some of Dad's colleagues about a possible merger."

"But it's Saturday," she said. "And the party..."

"We'll be back well in time for it, don't get overheated," he said with mild sarcasm.

She sighed. "Well, I guess business doesn't take holidays, does it?"

"No, it doesn't. I'll have Denny back in plenty of time," he said shortly.

She glanced at him, but he turned away to light a cigarette. He did that a lot when he was with her, but his ashtray was hardly used during the day when he was alone. She sighed. She was definitely a threat to his health.

"How are you going, on a charter flight?" she asked as she closed her overnight bag and checked to make sure everything in her apartment was turned off.

"No. We're flying up in the corporation's airplane."

She felt a twinge of fear, and gripped the small bag close as she turned. "The one your father almost crashed in a month ago?" she asked, recalling the day it had happened with vivid unease.

"It's been completely overhauled," he said curtly. "For God's sake, Denny's a big boy. What do you want to do, carry him up to South Carolina on your back?"

She couldn't tell him that her fear was all for him, that she didn't think she could go on living if anything happened to him. So she kept her mouth shut and followed him out the door. Anyway, she told herself, it would be all right.

For goodness sake, planes were safer than cars, weren't they?

As soon as they arrived at the house Regan went straight to the study, where his father and Denny were talking quietly. After the initial greetings were exchanged, Kenna turned to Denny. "Where's Margo?" she asked, noting the other woman's absence.

Denny smiled grimly. "She wasn't on the flight yesterday. I got a call from her last night. Long distance. She's decided to spend the extra week at home after all. I told her that was just as well, since I'd been spending a lot of time with you," Denny concluded with a wicked light in his eye. "We've had a great time together this week, haven't we, Kenna?"

Kenna groaned inwardly and made a face at Denny, knowing the effect his words would have on Regan.

But Regan wasn't looking at her expression, and he turned into the study. "I need to take another look at those contracts, Dad," he told his father.

Angus glanced from one of his sons to the other and shrugged. "All right. Denny?"

"I think I'll keep Kenna company," the younger man said.

"Have your mother bring us some coffee, will you?" Angus asked. He winked at Kenna and walked into the study. Regan glared at his stepbrother and Kenna before he slammed the door behind him.

"He's making a habit of that lately," Denny observed, grimacing.

"Oh, you should have stuck around yesterday afternoon," she told him as they walked into the kitchen, where Abbie was taking a tray of homemade cookies out of the oven.

"Why?" Abbie asked immediately, glancing toward Kenna with a wide-eyed grin. "What happened?"

"Mom, you're impossible," Denny told her, laughingly perching himself on the kitchen sink to watch her work.

"I always was, that's why your father married me. Come on, Kenna, spill the beans. Something very fishy is going on around here."

Kenna lifted both eyebrows. "Maybe you only smell your worms," she murmured.

"Stop that," Abbie admonished. She piled cookies on a platter with a spatula. "Regan drags Angus off into the study when they've already discussed those contracts six times.

Denny looks like the end of the world. You,'' she stared pointedly at Kenna's flushed face, ''look as if you'd like to take a bite out of something or somebody. And Margo,'' she glanced toward her youngest son, ''mysteriously lengthens her stay at home. And you tell me nothing is going on?''

''Why don't you write whodunnits?'' Denny suggested. ''You always have such suspicions. . . .''

''I only want to know one thing,'' Abbie persisted. ''Is it you and you,'' she glanced from one of them to the other, ''or is it another combination?''

''It's Denny and Margo,'' Kenna said with a smile. ''Or at least, they're hoping it is.''

''And where do you fit in?'' Abbie asked.

''I lost the glass slipper,'' came the wistful reply.

''Huh?'' the older woman said blankly.

''For your birthday, I'll tell you the whole story,'' Kenna promised. ''It's awfully complicated.''

''So I gathered.''

''Why do I get this feeling that I'm as much in the dark as you are?'' Denny asked Abbie with a frown.

"Probably because you are. Okay, honey, we'll stop ganging up on you," Abbie told Kenna and hugged her quickly. "But on my birthday, I'll expect you here with all your facts on the tip of your tongue."

"Yes, ma'am," Kenna said politely.

"Am I invited, too?" Denny asked.

"Ask your mother. Oh, Regan asked if he and his father could have some coffee in the study," Kenna added, just remembering.

"Asked?" Abbie scoffed. "The last time Regan asked for anything was when he had his appendix removed, and that courtesy only lasted until he got out from under the anesthetic. Here, Kenna, you take it to them."

Kenna looked hunted. Denny noticed her reluctance and stepped in.

"I'll do it," he said, lifting the tray. He winked at his mother. "It's too heavy for a mere woman."

"I'll sue," Kenna called after him. "But thanks."

"Anytime."

"Now," Abbie said, seeing her opportunity. "He's part of the problem, isn't he? You're head over heels in love with Regan, or I'm a white mouse."

Kenna sank down in a chair, looking utterly miserable. "You see, Regan was going to help me get Denny's attention—which I thought I wanted. So he took me shopping and got me this haircut," she indicated the short, flattering style, "and makeup and showed me what clothes to buy. Then he taught me how to walk and talk and flirt and act seductive. Then he sent me after Denny."

"The fairy godmother." Abbie grinned wickedly.

Kenna laughed despite her misery. "Fairy godfather," she corrected. "Anyway, now Denny's about to lose Margo because Regan was throwing me at him, and Regan walks around smoldering and looking purely hostile."

"I know that. But why?"

"He doesn't want to get involved, he says," Kenna sighed. She glanced up at Abbie, saw an ally, and decided to tell the whole truth. "He wants me, but he won't do anything about it because I'm still a virgin. And he doesn't want anything else, so . . ." She shrugged and hung her clasped hands between her knees. "Oh, damn it, Abbie. I hate men."

"So do I," the older woman agreed with a grimace. "I imagine he's afraid, Kenna. He did love Jessica obsessively. He's like that. He can't give a part of himself, he gives everything."

Kenna studied her fingernails. "She was lucky to be loved so much. I can't imagine a man caring about me that way."

"You might be very surprised. Here, honey, help me get these cookies into the fridge. Denny will be back any minute, and I don't think he needs any more ammunition to use against Regan. He's violently jealous of him, you know," Abbie sighed.

"Yes, I know, but he shouldn't be. He's quite a man himself," she said with a kind smile. "Why won't your husband give him a chance?"

"My husband," the older woman growled, "is a haughty, arrogant type who thinks he knows everything there is to know about personalities. But I'm working on him. So is Regan. We'll change his mind about Denny yet."

"I'd gladly put in my two cents' worth if I could," Kenna said on a sigh.

"Don't look so depressed, love," she said soothingly. "This is going to be a great party, even if I say so myself, and we'll dance and drink champagne and let the future take care of itself. Just take it one hour at a time.''

''I hope you're right, Abbie.''

''I hope you brought something eye-catching to use on Regan,'' Abbie grinned.

Kenna lifted her eyebrows and smiled back. ''I certainly did. Want to see it?''

''Yes, as a matter of fact, I do.'' She took off her apron and tossed it over the back of a chair. ''The caterers can take care of everything else. Come on, show me yours and I'll show you mine.''

''How long have you and Mr. Cole been married?'' Kenna asked as they mounted the carpeted staircase.

''Twenty-six years today,'' the shorter woman sighed. ''How time flies. And I still think Angus is the sexiest man I've ever known.''

Kenna couldn't imagine anyone thinking Angus Cole sexy. But probably Abbie still did. She wondered how she'd feel if she and Regan were celebrating their twenty-sixth wedding anniversary, and tingled all over at the thought. She knew she'd think he was sexy twenty-six years from now.

When she and Abbie came back downstairs, Denny and his father were in the study with the door open, and Regan was nowhere in sight.

"Where did he go?" Abbie asked, her voice lowered conspiratorially as the women joined the men.

"He's gone to get dressed," Angus offered, raising an eyebrow in Kenna's direction. "In a hurry to get away, it looks like. We've got another hour before we have to leave for the airport."

Denny was watching Kenna, too, and he drew her to one side while Angus and Abbie discussed the party arrangements.

"Regan gave me his blessing," he told Kenna with a sly grin. "Not generously, but he gave it to me, then he poured himself a slug of Dad's gin and went up to dress."

"Oh," Kenna said miserably, staring at her shoes.

"You don't understand," he persisted. "He hates gin. I don't think he knew what he was drinking. Why don't you go up and tell him I'm on the verge of proposing and see what happens?" He grinned. "I dare you."

"I've got bad vibrations about doing that," she said nervously.

"You never know until you try."

"That's true."

"Go on," he challenged. "What have you got to lose?"

"My pride, my self-respect, my..."

"Go, girl," he told her, turning her around. "I'm going to call Margo and see if she'll give up her neighbor and come home and marry me. We're both going to get it together before we quit. Now get in there and fight, troops!" he said with his old familiar enthusiasm.

She laughed helplessly. "He won't like it."

"Good. It will make him see what he's giving up."

She sighed. "All or nothing, huh?" She straightened the hem of her blouse and pursed her lips. "Wish me luck."

"Will you need it, looking the way you do?" Denny asked.

"That reminds me. Here." She tugged off her glasses and handed them to him, and smoothed her hair. "Point me toward the staircase, please."

"Right there. Up the stairs and first door to the right."

"Thanks, partner."

She marched up the long staircase with her heart hammering in her throat. Please, let it work, she prayed silently. Let him care. Let him be insanely jealous and tell me not to go near Denny again!

She walked up to his door and hesitated. Well, Denny was right, what did she have to lose? And she was the one who'd been lecturing Regan about daring to live. . . .

She knocked firmly on his door.

"What is it?" he growled.

"Could I talk to you for a minute?" she called through the heavy wood.

There was a pregnant pause, and she stood nervously outside in the hall, wondering what she'd do if he said no. But after a minute she heard heavy footsteps, and then the door swung open.

She wasn't prepared at all for the sight that met her shocked eyes. She'd seen Regan in his shirt sleeves, but that was as disheveled as he'd ever been in her company. Until now. He was stripped to the waist, and Kenna wondered if it was acceptable for a modern woman to faint at such sights. He was the most gorgeous-looking thing she'd ever seen. The pickiest connoisseur of men's bare chests couldn't have found a flaw in him. He was heavily muscled, bronzed and fit, and there was a wedge of thick black hair curling from his collarbone down to his belt, and probably far below that. Kenna had to clench her hands at her sides to keep them from making a grab for him.

"Well?" he asked curtly.

She dragged her eyes up to meet his and forgot everything she'd come upstairs to say.

He had a towel in one hand, apparently having just come from a shower, because his dark, shaggy hair was still damp. But if he was irritated because she'd interrupted him, it didn't show.

Wordlessly, he caught her clenched hand and dragged her into the room, closing the door quietly behind them. His eyes searched hers for a long, static moment before he abruptly tossed the towel into a nearby chair and brought both her hands to his broad chest.

"Well?" he asked quietly.

It was all she could do to answer him. She could think of nothing but the feel of that thick, cool mass of hair under her fingers. She had to force her hands not to start anything by caressing him as they ached to.

"Denny's asked me . . . to marry him," she said, giving the lie straightforwardly as Denny had suggested.

His chest rose and fell heavily under her hands. She closed her eyes and wished with all her heart that he loved her as much as she loved him, that he'd tell her so and carry her the few feet to the brown-patterned bedspread and lay her down on it. . . .

Her heart throbbed wildly when he suddenly lifted her clear of the floor and did almost that. He carried her to the bed and dropped her into its softness, throwing himself down with her. His arms supported him as he poised himself above her.

"Is this what you want?" he asked coldly. "One last fling with me before you give him an answer? Why not? Maybe we can get each other out of our systems before you start wearing his ring . . ." Before he finished the sentence, his mouth was crushing down against hers.

She stiffened, but only for a minute. She'd waited too long, wanted him too long, to protest. Burying her pride, she reached up and touched him, feeling the smooth texture of his bronzed skin, tugging at the thick hair over his chest, exploring every hard muscle with fingers that trembled with hunger. Her mouth opened without any coaxing, her tongue answered the hard thrust of his. Her body seemed to curl up with pleasure at the sweet, wild intimacy they were sharing.

"Is this what you want?" he asked against her mouth, and his voice was unsteady.

"Yes," she whispered unashamedly. Her arms reached up to bring him even closer. "Oh, yes, this is what I want, Regan."

His mouth brushed against hers softly, feeling its silky texture, while his fingers went down to the front of her blouse and began to methodically unfasten the buttons one by one.

She knew what he was doing, but she didn't make a sound or try to stop him. Her body belonged to him, as it could never belong to any other man. If he wanted it now, he was welcome to it. She wasn't going to fight.

"No fuss, Cinderella?" he asked when he freed the last button and eased the edges apart, baring the lacy little bra she wore under the blouse.

"No fuss," she whispered, watching his face as he reached under her to unclasp the bra and tug it loose.

He lifted her, deftly sliding the blouse down one arm and then the other. The straps of the bra followed, and when he lowered her back to the bed, there was nothing between his dark, quiet eyes and her body.

She tried to breathe normally, but her heart was beating madly. She caressed his dark face with her eyes, fascinated by the expression that had claimed it as he looked down at her small, taut breasts.

"Are you disappointed?" she asked softly.

"No." He brushed his fingers over her collarbone and lifted his eyes to meet hers. "No, I'm not disappointed." he watched her as his hand moved, lightly stroking her smooth flesh. He caught the hard peak between his fingers and tugged gently at it, and she arched and caught her breath at the aching pleasure.

Her fingers clung to his hard arms and she stared at him like a tiny wounded thing, helpless in the hands of its captor. But it wasn't a wound she felt, it was a kind of pleasure she'd only heard about until now.

"Lift up, darling," he whispered, moving his hands around her to bring her body up against his bare chest. "Let me show you how it feels," he breathed, watching her softness disappear into the tangle of hair over his warm chest. "Oh, God, I never dreamed anything could be so sweet!"

She caught her breath and pressed close, shutting her eyes to savor the wild magic of this new intimacy. She slid her arms around his neck and burrowed her face into his throat, while he eased onto his side and brought her completely against his powerful body. Her legs brushed his, feeling their strength, her hips arched against him and felt the immediate response of his body to the soft contact.

"Regan," she whispered drowsily, her voice hungry and soft with love.

"I could take you now," he whispered roughly. His hands slid down her sides, brushing her breasts, and still further down until they found the base of her spine.

His leg edged between hers and his mouth sought hers again, taking it with a lazy, insistent pressure that dragged a moan from her throat. His hands were smoothing her skin, finding the gentle rise of her body with reverence in their touch.

He bit at her mouth softly and drew away. "I want to kiss you here," he murmured, emphasizing the whisper with his hands. "You're

like velvet, so soft to touch.'' He eased her
onto her back and looked down at her body,
his face unreadable, his eyes blazing.

She arched her back like a cat being stroked,
faintly shocked at her own abandon. She
wasn't embarrassed with him or shy or even
self-conscious. She loved the feel of his eyes,
his hands. It was so beautiful with him.

His fingers caught her waist, pressing into it
to test its taut perfection. They moved over her
flat stomach, around to her back and lifted her
to his mouth.

She trembled, and an odd little sound sur-
faced as she felt for the first time the magic of
a man's warm mouth on her soft flesh.

''I could make a meal of you,'' he whispered quietly. ''Every time I touch you, I go a
little mad.''

Her fingers stroked his dark, cool hair and
her eyes closed on wave after wave of sweet
pleasure. ''So do I,'' she whispered back. She
arched, forcing her body closer to his seeking
lips. ''This is beautiful,'' she managed unsteadily. ''So . . . very beautiful.''

''Come closer, Kenna,'' he whispered. His
mouth slid up to cover hers, and he folded her

into the curve of his body, so that they were closer than they'd ever been.

She answered the soft hunger of his mouth with a response that dragged a groan from his taut body. His hands at her back trembled slightly, and his hips moved against hers with a strange rhythm.

"No," he ground out suddenly. His body stilled and he crushed her for an instant before he let her go and rolled away. He sat up, swinging his legs off the bed, and bent his head into his hands. "No, Kenna."

She lay against the pillows, dazed with delightful sensations, staring at him. Her breath trembled into her throat. "Regan?" she whispered.

He drew in a harsh breath. "I can't," he bit off. "Don't you understand, damn it? I can't!"

Her lips trembled. The rejection was so complete that it hurt. She forced herself to sit up, to tug her bra and top back on without saying anything.

He got to his feet and pulled a cigarette from the pack on the chest of drawers, lighting it with hands that could hardly hold the flame steady. Then he went to the window and stared down at the rose garden it overlooked with blank eyes.

"It's because I'm not Jessica, isn't it?" she asked, getting unsteadily to her feet. "Because nobody can ever take her place with you."

He turned, scowling at her. "What the hell are you talking about?" he demanded harshly. "Don't start trying to shift the blame, honey, you're the one who came in here after me."

"Yes, I did," she admitted, "but you're the one who carried me to bed!"

"Were you protesting?" he asked. "I didn't notice any maidenly reservations. Just don't get the idea that once you're married I'll be willing to supply what Denny apparently can't," he added coldly.

Her face flamed. "I hope you can type, counselor, because after that crack, you'll be doing you own damned petitions from now on!"

"Quitting, are you?" he asked.

"Yes," she returned recklessly. "Denny's going to ask his father to let him work at the corporation, and I'm going, too! You can have the office all to yourself!"

"I won't need it," he said, turning back to the window. "I'm going back to New York next week. Denny and Dad and I settled it a few minutes ago."

She wanted to sit down in the middle of the floor and cry. Just for an instant, she considered it, if only to see what he'd do. He'd probably walk over her, she thought miserably.

With her heart around her ankles, along with her pride, she turned to open the door.

"I'm sorry I caused you to compromise your principles," she said bitterly. "I won't throw myself at you again."

"The blame isn't all yours," he said wearily. "I can't seem to keep my hands away from you lately. I didn't mean for that to happen."

"I know." Tears were welling up in her eyes. "When will you leave?"

"Monday," he said firmly. "That attempted murder case I told you about comes up on the calendar the following week, and I need that time. I don't intend to lose."

"When have you ever lost a case?" she asked with bitter humor. "I hope you get a conviction, counselor."

"You and Denny," he said, "remember to invite me to the wedding."

"Sure," she choked, careful to keep her back to him. "Thanks again for all the help. I'll pay you back for the clothes just as soon..."

"Consider them a wedding gift," he said curtly. "I hope Denny will make you happy."

I'm not going to marry Denny, and he'll never make me happy. I'll grieve all my life for love of you, she thought in anguish. But she only nodded, and kept the damning words to herself.

"We won't talk again," he said as she opened the door. "Not like this. I hope we'll part as friends, Kenna."

She couldn't look at him. "You'll always be my friend," she said quietly. "As long as I'm alive."

"Are you crying?" he asked suddenly.

"No, of course not." She walked through the doorway. "I think I'd like to go home after the party. I'll get Denny to drive me, you won't have to."

"You don't have to go that far to avoid me," he said roughly. "Stay. I'll go back to Atlanta myself."

Tears burst over the dam of her lower lids and spilled onto her cheeks. "Damn you," she choked, "crawl into the grave with her and see if I care!"

She ran down the hall as if the hounds of hell were after her, ignoring the harsh sound of her name on his lips as he called after her. She went into her own room and slammed the door, locking it. And she stayed there until she was sure Denny and Regan had gone.

Chapter Nine

The day dragged after the two men had gone. Kenna tried to stay out of the way when the caterers arrived to start their own preparations for the evening. The florist delivered the arrangements Abbie had ordered, and Angus busied himself in the study while Kenna helped Abbie with last minute touches in the living room.

The tables were lovely—covered with white linen and Abbie's best silver, dotted with fresh flower arrangements and trays waiting to be filled. The kitchen was alive with the caterers as they began to prepare the evening's canapés and finger foods.

Abbie rushed around trying to get everything together, but as the afternoon wore on she began to look troubled.

She checked her watch as she joined Kenna in the living room for a quick cup of coffee. "They should be calling from the airport by now," she murmured. "Oh, where are they? The guests will be here in just a few hours...Kenna, men have no consideration whatsoever," she grumbled just before she got up and started back to the kitchen. "And they say women are bad about spending hours talking."

Kenna only smiled. "They'll be here soon," she said confidently, trying not to think about the fact that the airplane had already malfunctioned once....

To take her mind off her own worry, Kenna strolled around the grounds with Pooch. He followed her lazily, pausing occasionally to bark at shadows in the woods. She tossed a crust of bread to the swans at the edge of the lake and let her mind drift to more pleasant thoughts. At least she'd have something of Regan to remember when he went back to New York. A scrapbook of sweet dreams and bits of happiness to tuck away in the back of her mind and bring out on lonely winter nights.

If only he could have put away his grief. She would have helped him. Not that she'd want him to forget Jessica entirely. Love came in so many forms, each one subtly different and special. It was possible to love more than once, and she couldn't begrudge Jessica the part of his life she'd shared. He was the kind of man who deserved to be loved deeply and completely. What a pity that he'd decided he could do without love for the rest of his life.

She ruffled Pooch's fur and they started back to the house. Abbie was just coming down the tree-lined path, looking for her, with trouble written on her like a slogan.

"What's wrong?" Kenna asked without preliminaries, already fearing the worst.

"The plane went down," Abbie said hoarsely.

Kenna stood frozen in the middle of the path, while the world seemed to blacken and die around her. No, it couldn't be.

"The plane?" she echoed blankly.

"Yes," Abbie said, going close to hug Kenna to her. "Oh, Kenna, they've crashed in the damned thing,'' she moaned, breaking down completely. ''My sons, my boys . . . !''

And now Kenna had to believe, because she'd never seen Abbie Cole cry. Numbly, her arms enfolded the shorter woman and she felt a cold ache inside as the full impact hit her. The plane had gone down. It had crashed. With Regan and Denny inside. Regan might be dead.

She couldn't remember ever feeling so full of terror. It came over her like a black sickness, blinding her with tears.

''Oh, no,'' she whispered, as if words could stop the nightmare before it began. ''No.''

''Damned plane,'' Abbie growled in anguish, her voice breaking. ''Damned, damned plane! They promised us it was safe . . . !''

Kenna soothed her with hands that felt numb from cold and shock. ''How did it happen?''

''We don't know.'' Abbie pulled away and wiped at her eyes with a big handkerchief before she handed it to Kenna, who hadn't realized that huge teardrops were rolling down her own pale cheeks. ''All we know is that they left Greenville hours ago. When they didn't arrive at the airport, the airport operator called us.

He's a close friend, you see. He called the Greenville airport to see when they'd filed their flight plan and when they'd left. The mountains...and it's raining. Oh, my God, why did they have to call that stupid meeting today, of all days? My anniversary...!''

"It will be all right," Kenna said quietly, using the routine words that people said at times like this. Words that didn't mean a damned thing.

"I hope so, Kenna," Abbie groaned. "I hope so! Come on; we're going out to the airport. I can't sit here and wait for telephone calls; I've got to be where I can find out something."

Angus was already pulling his car keys out of his pocket when they got back to the house, his face hard and grim and so much like Regan's that Kenna burst into fresh tears.

"Regan was flying," Angus told the women as they got into his Mercedes and started for the airport. "He's level-headed at the controls; he's flown combat missions. If it was possible to bring that plane down in one piece, he'd have done it."

"Pilot error accounts for most accidents," Abbie agreed, "but equipment failure accounts for its share. And that damned plane's already gone down once," she reminded her husband with trembling lips.

Kenna, sitting in the back seat with fear numbing her body, listened without trying to join in the conversation. Regan, she whispered, oh, God, please let Regan be alive, please don't let him die. Please don't let him die.

"If they walk away from this one, I'll have that machine taken apart piece by piece and melted down," Angus promised curtly.

"Do they have any idea, any at all, where it might have gone down?" Abbie was asking. "Those mountains around Toccoa, or near Robertstown..."

"That would have been off their flight path," Angus murmured.

"Yes, but it's raining; they might have been blown off course. Or if their instruments malfunctioned...Angus, I can't bear to lose them both," she broke down. "Oh, God, I've covered so many plane crashes! I know too much about what happens, things that never get into print because they're too horrible."

"Stop it," Angus said quietly. "Just calm down and stop thinking the worst. Don't borrow trouble, darling."

"I'm sorry." Abbie dabbed at her eyes and turned to look back at Kenna. "Are you all right?"

Kenna nodded. "Will it be a long time, before we know?"

Angus shrugged. "I don't know," he said with suppressed emotion in his deep voice. His hands tightened on the steering wheel. "Maybe we'll get lucky."

"Our anniversary," Abbie murmured miserably, and sniffed back fresh tears. "I told the caterers to take care of the guests if we're not back; it's too late to cancel. And I . . . I just can't start phoning people now. . . ."

"One step at a time, Abbie," Angus said gently. He reached over and caught his wife's hand in his and held it firmly. "We'll wait and pray and hope for the best."

"Yes, Angus," the tearful woman agreed, returning the pressure with her own fingers.

Kenna, watching them, began to understand what Abbie saw in the older man. He's like Regan, she thought. He's strong and gentle and like a rock when she needs someone to lean on. That brought the tears back, and she dragged a tissue from her purse.

Later, she huddled next to Abbie on the bare wood bench outside the airport office, watching the gray skies with eyes that didn't even see. Despite the fact that the plane was overdue and very likely down somewhere, Abbie couldn't stop herself from looking for it. Greenville was only a little less than a two hour drive from Gainesville; it was hardly any distance at all. How could it have happened? The thunderstorm might have driven them off course, but the airport manager said that they hadn't radioed in. The Atlanta Flight Service had phoned him when the twin-engine plane was overdue, and a telephone search had resulted as they called airport after airport looking for the missing pilot and his passenger.

"We're going to be soaked if we stay out here, I guess," Abbie said, "but I'll be damned if I can go inside and listen..." Her voice broke and she burst into tears again. "I can't bear to lose them," she confessed.

Kenna hugged her close with a sob. "Neither can I," she confessed. Her lower lip trembled and the runway blurred in front of her eyes. "Abbie, if anything happens to him, I don't think I can bear to go on living."

The older woman drew back to look into Kenna's tormented eyes. "Regan?" she asked.

Kenna nodded. "Regan."

"My dear," Abbie said helplessly. She put her arms around the younger woman and they sat there in the rain, comforting each other, while the skies darkened and the mist settled around them.

Angus brought them cups of steaming black coffee. "It will be dark soon," he said. "They won't start searching until tomorrow morning, if it comes to that." He shrugged his broad shoulders as he scanned the skies. "Even if they went down safely, it would probably take time to get to a telephone. There are lots of rural areas between here and Greenville...."

"Yes, that's true," Abbie said numbly. "But there are lots of hilly places—the mountains to the west."

"Come inside, both of you," Angus said gently. "You'll have pneumonia, sitting out here."

"I can't stand it in there," Kenna whispered.

"Neither can I," Abbie agreed. "You'll call us . . . ?"

"Angus!" the airport manager called. "In here!"

Angus paused, as if he would have liked to protect the women from what he might hear, as if he wanted to forbid them to come in with him. But Abbie and Kenna were already on their feet, looking as if they'd fight him if he tried to stop them. He shrugged, and drew them into the office with him.

The manager was laughing. Laughing! "They're fine," he said without preamble, a microphone in one hand. "Regan got the plane down okay, but they've had a cold, wet wait for the rescuers. He landed it in a cow pasture in northeast Georgia."

"What the hell happened?" Angus demanded, fear giving way to anger.

"The instrument panel caught fire and they had to put down. Regan managed to ditch in time, so that the emergency location transmitter remained intact. But their navigation equipment had been damaged and they were way off course. A private plane caught the signal and relayed it to ground rescue units." He grinned. "Would you like me to tell you the odds against landing a twin-engine plane in a cow pasture? Good thing he flew fighters in Nam, wasn't it, Angus?''

Angus was laughing, but there were tears of relief in his eyes. "Good thing," he admitted. He paused to catch his breath. "Where are they now?"

"On their way here," the operator said, grinning. "An old flying buddy of mine's bringing them down in his own plane."

Kenna was crying quietly, along with Abbie, and she offered up a silent prayer of thanks. The light had come back into her life. Despite the rain and gloom of the past few hours, it was beautiful to be alive and in the same world with Regan. Even if she never saw him again, that would be all right now. He was alive. Thank God, he was alive.

The next half an hour seemed to take forever, while Kenna drank black coffee with the others and scanned the dark skies with eyes that were hungry for sight of a beloved face. She was bedraggled and wet through and through. One of the airport people had loaned her his sweater, and Abbie had Angus's jacket, but Kenna didn't even feel the cold.

When the single-engine plane landed and taxied to a stop on the apron, Kenna started running toward it. She didn't care anymore about her stupid pride or keeping secrets. She loved Regan, and she didn't care if it showed, she didn't care who knew it. Nothing mattered now except touching him and holding him, and making sure that he was really alive and not just a figment of her tortured imagination. She was hardly aware of Abbie and Angus behind her, of other people.

Regan and Denny came out of the plane and stood together, watching her run toward them. They looked as wet as she did. Regan's face had some cuts, and his jacket was torn; Denny was holding his arm. But they were alive.

"Regan!" Kenna cried, sounding like someone returning from hell.

She ran straight to him, hardly seeing Denny or the shocked expression in Regan's dark eyes as he opened his arms for her.

Her body hit his with the impact of a blow. Her arms reached up to cling as she held him with every ounce of strength in her trembling body. Her eyes closed on a flood of tears. He was safe. He felt warm and solid and she could feel his breath at her ear. He was safe.

His arms contracted hungrily, painfully at her back, bruising her against his big body. His face nuzzled urgently against hers as he sought her mouth and found it. They kissed hungrily, taking each other's mouths with a hot, wild anguish that took them far away from the drizzle and the curious stares. She clung, feeling him tremble, loving the bruising abandon of his big arms, the devouring pressure of his mouth biting into hers.

She didn't see Denny hugging his parents, she wasn't aware of Angus's hand touching Regan's back, of Abbie's loving stare. Her whole being had concentrated itself into showing Regan how glad she was that he was alive. That he was home.

A long, long minute later he lifted his head. His eyes were glittering with an odd wildness as he looked down at her, and he was trembling from head to toe. So was she, but for a different reason altogether, she imagined. She let her arms slide away from him, but she couldn't drag her eyes from his.

Her fingers touched his face. "You're hurt," she whispered on a sob.

"No," he said in a strangely shaken tone, "it's just a cut."

"We were so worried," Abbie interrupted, taking the opportunity to hug him. "Landing a plane in a cow pasture. That's a new one."

"It was hairy for a few minutes," Denny chuckled, looking from Kenna's white face to Regan's darkly flushed one. "But Regan's combat training came in handy. Uh, Dad, the plane . . ."

"Damn the plane," Angus grumbled, shaking Regan's hand warmly. "We'll melt down what's left of it and buy a new one."

"Thank God we had those life jackets up front with us," Denny remarked. "We used them to cushion our faces from the impact."

"Is your arm broken?" Angus asked his youngest son.

"I don't think so, but we'd both better stop by the emergency room at the hospital and have ourselves checked," Denny sighed. "We're both a little banged up."

"We'll do that," Angus agreed. "You've got ten days to write a report on this to file with the National Transportation Safety Board."

"I phoned them before we left to fly down here," Regan told his father. "They're mailing me the forms."

He sounded shaken, but Kenna supposed he had a right to be. She was looking at him with eyes so wide with fear and relief and concern that Abbie had to stifle a telling remark.

"We'd better go," Angus murmured. "Fellas, you'll never know how much we appreciate your help," he began, moving into the throng of airport personnel to express his gratitude.

"Are you all right?" Abbie asked Denny, putting a supporting arm around him.

"I'm fine," he said with a grin.

Kenna belatedly moved away from Regan to hug Denny. "I'm sorry you were hurt," she said numbly. "But I'm so glad you're both alive."

"I'll be back in a minute," Regan said quietly and walked into the office where Angus had gone.

"You gave the show away, you know," Denny murmured with a wry smile as he looked down at Kenna. "You can't go around kissing men that way unless you're pretty involved emotionally, and Regan isn't stupid."

She sighed with a weary smile. "Isn't it a good thing he's going back to New York?" she asked miserably. "I won't have him giving me pitying looks."

"If the way he kissed you just now was pity," Abbie murmured, "I'm a duck."

"He didn't have much choice, since I was doing the kissing," Kenna said. She brushed the hair away from her eyes. "It doesn't matter, anyway. I'd rather have the two of you alive than have my pride intact."

"Amen." Abbie grinned. "Come on, let's get you to the emergency room."

"The party," Denny burst out, just remembering.

"I'm sure the guests are having a great time," Abbie said carelessly. "So will we, when we get there. What a nice anniversary present you are, my darling," she added, and reached up to kiss him with a smile.

Denny only laughed and kissed her back.

It was crowded in the Mercedes going home. The emergency room doctor had put an ace bandage around Denny's sprained wrist and treated the cuts on Regan's dark face. After which, he had given them both a clean bill of health. Kenna was sandwiched in between the two men, feeling Regan's hard thigh against her leg and his shoulder brushing hers.

If she'd embarrassed him, it didn't show. But he didn't speak, letting Denny tell the harrowing story of the ditching.

It was enough for Kenna to sit beside him. So little a thing to give so much pleasure. She leaned back against the seat and closed her eyes, while the conversation around her buzzed in her ears without making sense.

The house was full of curious people, none of whom Kenna recognized. They came forward as the Coles walked in the door, and Angus briefly explained what had happened.

"Anyway," he told the guests, "the excitement's over, and if you'll excuse us for just a minute while we change clothes, we'll be right with you. We've sure got something to celebrate now!"

And he led the way upstairs. Kenna quickly changed into her evening gown and ran a brush through her short hair. She put on a light coat of pale lipstick and gave thanks all over again that Regan was alive. That both men were, she corrected silently. Well, he knew the truth now, she thought miserably. Everybody knew it.

With a sinking heart, she went back down to join the others. This would surely be the last time she'd see Regan. That would probably be the best thing for both of them. It would be as much of an embarrassment to him as it would be to her, to have everyone know she was wearing her heart on her sleeve for him.

Abbie was standing apart from Angus in the family room, a glass of champagne in her hand.

"Have some, dear," she said to Kenna, lifting a filled glass from the table. "I poured it for you."

"Thank you." She searched the room. "Where's Denny?"

"On the phone. With Margo," she added with a grin. "She just called, and he's regaling her with tales of his bravery. Isn't it great?"

She laughed. "Oh, yes, it is. I think he's hooked this time, you know."

"Well, she'll be a handful," Abbie observed. "But I like her well enough, and she is easy on the eyes. And we have the satisfaction of knowing she isn't after his money. That bothered all of us, before we found out about her background."

Kenna nodded, staring into her glass. She tended to forget how wealthy the family was. They didn't flaunt what they had, or act superior to other people.

"That sounded terrible, didn't it?" Abbie said gruffly, touching Kenna's arm lightly. "I sound as if I'm immediately suspicious of every woman who looks at my sons. Kenna, no one who saw you with Regan this afternoon could ever accuse you of being a gold digger. Do you know, I've never seen people kiss that way—except myself and Angus, years ago. I knew everything you were feeling. And it wasn't a sudden thirst for money."

"I knew you didn't mean me," Kenna said quietly. She glanced up and looked at Regan, filled with love and gratitude for his safety. As if he sensed that searching stare, he looked up into her eyes. And time seemed to stop around them for a space of seconds until he looked back at his father.

"He thought you were going to marry Denny," Abbie said abruptly.

"Did he?" She sipped her drink.

"Was he supposed to think that?"

She nodded. "We, uh, thought it might make him jealous." Tears clouded her eyes. "Wasn't that funny?" She turned away. "I don't think I can stand any more tonight. Would you be terribly offended if I said good night and went to bed?"

"But it's barely ten o'clock, darling," Abbie protested gently. "You haven't danced one dance," she added, nodding toward the couples moving to the delightful sound of a small combo that had been hired for the occasion.

"I don't really feel like it." She put down her half finished glass of champagne and hugged Abbie impulsively. "I'm glad they're both safe. See you in the morning, okay?"

"Okay. Sleep well, my dear."

"You, too. Uh, will you...tell the others?" she asked nervously, dreading a confrontation if she had to do it herself.

Abbie nodded understandingly. "Of course I will. Want some aspirin?"

"No. Just a warm bath and my bed. Are we all going to church in the morning?" she added.

Abbie smiled. "You bet. You can borrow a dress from me if you didn't bring one."

She returned the smile. "I did. 'Night."

She turned and walked quickly out of the room, oblivious to the dark eyes that followed her path with mingled confusion and hunger.

Chapter Ten

Kenna stretched out in the blue bathtub with a sigh, letting the warm water surround her with the delicate lilac scent she'd added to it. It felt so good to let her aching muscles relax.

She lathered and rinsed and arched her back as she trailed water down it to wash the soap away. And that was when she became aware of someone in the room with her.

She opened her eyes and turned her head toward the door. Shock froze her in place for an instant, and Regan took full advantage of it to look down at her soft, pink bareness with dark, possessive eyes.

Apparently, he'd given up on the party, too, because his white frilled shirt was open all the way down the front and all he had on with it was his slacks.

"I'm taking a bath," Kenna managed in a high-pitched, breathless tone as she tried to decide what to do. The washcloth would hardly be of any use at all, and he was standing next to her towel.

"Yes, I can see that," he said gently. He smiled at her, the first genuine smile she could remember on his hard face in a long time. "My God, you're a delight to the eyes."

She flushed at the compliment and waited there, sitting up, in a flurry of confusion.

"Stand up," he said quietly. "I'll dry you."

He pulled the towel from the rack and she tried to decide between diving under the water or making a run for it.

That indecision must have shown, because he laughed softly. "There's nothing to be embarrassed about, darling," he said, moving closer with the towel raised. "You're beautiful, and I love looking at you. Now stand up. You can't stay in there."

He made it seem so natural. Her own reaction startled her, because she got gracefully to her feet and stepped out onto the bath mat, searching his quiet face with wide, curious eyes.

"You see," he said quietly, wrapping her in the towel, "there's nothing to be ashamed of. Nudity is beautiful. It's the distortions people make of it that bring shame."

Her eyes searched his face, lingering on the deep cut beside his jaw. She reached up and touched it gently where the antiseptic stopped. "I'd never been so afraid in my life as I was when Abbie told me the plane was lost," she said involuntarily. Tears sprang to her eyes with remembered terror.

"I could see that for myself, Kenna," he murmured. He dried her slowly, gently, and tossed the towel aside to swing her up in his big arms. "I can't tell you how I felt when you ran to me instead of Denny at the airport. My God, I almost cried...."

She buried her face in his throat, feeling the warmth and strength of him like a brand against her bareness. Involuntarily, she pulled his opened shirt aside to press her body against the hair-matted muscle and gasped at the sweet contact.

"I love you," she breathed, dragging her breasts against him slowly, with an aching hunger. "I love you, and I don't care if the whole world knows it . . . !"

"I imagine most of it does, if they saw the way you kissed me at the airport," he murmured huskily. "Don't be so aggressive, baby, you'll make me lose control."

"I want you to lose control," she whispered in his ear. "I want you to make love to me. I want to belong to you. I don't care if all I can ever have is tonight," she added, clinging, as her voice broke. "I love you . . . !"

His mouth slid across her cheek and onto her lips, stopping the words, taking possession with a slow, sweet intimacy that made her moan under its expertness.

"Be quiet," he whispered tenderly. He carried her into the adjoining bedroom and laid her down on the bed. He watched her closely as he drew his shirt off and tossed it onto a nearby chair. His slacks followed, and she averted her eyes as he joined her on the bed.

He turned her face back to his with a slow smile. "I doubt you can see this far, anyway, without your glasses," he remarked affectionately. "Not that it matters. You'd better get used to looking at me. I don't think people need to hide lovemaking in the darkness, like a guilty secret."

"It isn't that," she said breathlessly. "It's just that it's new territory for me."

"For me, too," he sighed, and looked down the length of her with a long, possessive appraisal. "You're going to be my first virgin."

That was shocking, and the look on her face told him so.

"Jessica had been married before," he said quietly. "And before we go any further, I want you to understand something. She was a part of my life that no longer exists. I loved her. But she's dead and I'm not and life goes on." He touched her face with a lightly caressing movement of his fingers, and his eyes glowed with some deep emotion. "You don't know beans about taking precautions, do you?" he asked suddenly, and grinned at the flaming blush on her face. "Never mind. If you get pregnant, it won't be the end of the world."

Her face was deep red, but she didn't look away. "You won't have to feel guilty about it...."

"Don't be absurd," he interrupted. He ran his hand down her body and watched her tremble with reaction. "We're going to be very good together. I knew that the day I walked into Denny's office for the first time and sparks flew between us. I fought you hard, honey. I was even willing to throw you at Denny's innocent head to save myself. But it all misfired.'' His face clouded. ''When you came in here this morning and told me he'd proposed, I think I went a little crazy. It was all I could do not to throw a punch at him when we left for the airport. I gave him hell all day, and he just sat there and grinned at me. When you came flying into my arms at the airport, I began to understand what was going on.''

She arched close to him, gasping as she felt the impact of his skin against every inch of hers. She nuzzled her face into his throat and let him feel the trembling of her body.

''I didn't have any pride left by then,'' she whispered shakily. ''I was scared silly. I still am.''

''Is that why you're trembling?'' he murmured wickedly. He let his hands run down her back to press her even closer. ''It's contagious, too,'' he added as his own body began to answer that wild shudder.

''I won't ask you for anything,'' she whispered. ''I . . . I have to be independent.''

He folded her close and kissed her flushed face, light, tender kisses that belied the hunger she could feel growing in his big, taut body.

"You can be independent to a certain point," he agreed. "But I'll want you with me when I travel. I don't want to spend nights away from you."

She found it increasingly hard to think as his hands began to move in strange, sweet patterns on her body, exploring her with an expertise that was at once embarrassing and wildly sensuous.

"You...you want us to be together more than just...on weekends?" she asked, tingling all over at the thought of being with him every night. Even if it only lasted for a few weeks, it would be all of heaven.

"Um-hmmm," he agreed, bending his head to drag his lips over her breasts, lingering on the taut peaks until she moaned wildly.

"For how long, though?" she managed. Her body was getting out of control, going its own way with a reckless abandon that startled her.

"Oh, fifty years or so," he murmured against her warm, flat stomach. "Maybe a few more than that...."

"Fifty years?" she burst out.

He lifted his head and arched an eyebrow at her. "Well, that's a pretty conservative guess, of course," he told her. "What with all these damned wonder drugs... Will you lie down and stop interrupting me? I thought you wanted to make love."

"I do... but...?"

"It's going to be love, too, Kenna," he said, and all the humor was gone out of his face, leaving it quiet and tender. He moved over her, resting his weight on his forearms to study her face while he shifted his warm, abrasive chest across her softness and smiled shamelessly at her helpless response. "It's going to be the sweetest, wildest expression of love you've ever imagined."

Her eyes were wide with love and passion and she was just barely hearing him. She felt an ache that had nothing to do with sore muscles.

"I love you, didn't you know?" he asked, holding her eyes. "Never more than when I thought I'd lost you to Denny, and I walked out the door hurting in so many ways that I didn't know how I was going to live. You will marry me, won't you?"

Tears sprang to her eyes. "Yes. Oh yes! I'd follow you barefooted through the snow," she whispered brokenly, "if you wanted me to."

"I know that," he said roughly. "I'd do the same for you. My God, I love you!"

Her arms reached up to bring him down to her. "Show me," she whispered tearfully. "And teach me how to show you."

He bent slowly to touch his open mouth to hers. "What a sweet thought," he whispered ardently. "Don't be nervous. I'm going to treat you like three-hundred-year-old china."

She tangled her trembling hands in his thick, dark hair. "I only want to please you," she whispered against the increasing intimacy of his lips.

"You will," he whispered. "And I'll please you, if it takes all night."

His hands touched her gently, in new ways, in wildly pleasing ways, until the flames burned high and bright and beautiful. And he watched her the whole time, his dark eyes tender and loving as he took her with him on a roller coaster. All the books Kenna had read hadn't prepared her for the sensations she learned as he eased her again and again into a perfect frenzy of pleasure only to calm her and soothe her and start over again. Time dissolved into a kaleidoscope of movement and urgent whispers and a pleasure that bordered on agony, until his incredible control finally gave out. She learned the mystery of total possession in such a storm of hunger that she didn't even notice whether there was pain.

Later, lying spent, her face wet with her own tears, she snuggled against his damp, pulsating chest, and could barely believe where she'd been. He was propped up on the pillows, looking down at her, and finally she was able to slide her head down his arm far enough to see his face.

"You liar," she whispered, shaken. "Only a few wild oats, my foot! Where did you learn how to do that? Never mind," she added quickly, touching his lips to keep the words back, "I don't want to know."

He arched an eyebrow. "Well, you said yourself that God compensated me for being ugly, didn't you?"

She laughed wearily, delightedly, smoothing the dark hair away from his broad forehead. "Oh, my darling, you'll never be ugly. Not to me. I love every break in your nose, and your big feet, and your ferocious scowl, and your temper...."

"You could have stopped at loving me, you know," he murmured lazily, "without enumerating my bad points."

"And I haven't even gotten to the best part," she grinned, blushing wildly as she realized how that sounded.

He laughed delightedly, and folded her against his side. "Imp. Delightful imp. Did I hurt you very much?"

"That's what I've been trying to tell you," she confessed, nuzzling her face against his. "I don't know. I really don't know, I was so out of my mind...Regan, will it always be like this for us, even when we're old and wrinkled?"

"Speak for yourself, I don't plan to get old. Just better. I'll improve with age." He kissed her softly. "So will you. We'll just better away together."

She laughed softly. "Or love away. I adore you."

"I adore you."

She sighed and stretched. "I'm so sleepy... do you suppose it will shock the household if you stay all night?"

"Dad will give us amused looks, Denny will grin, and Abbie will ask when I expect to make an honest woman of you. But no one will be shocked. They already know how it is with us. I think they knew before we did." He crushed out the cigarette in the ashtray by the bed and turned off the light. "You'd better sleep while you can. I have plans for you around dawn."

She giggled delightedly and snuggled close as he pulled the covers over them. She drank in the fragrance of his big body and drowned in love and the glory of sharing it. Her eyes opened, seeking him in the dim light from the moon outside the window.

"Regan?" she asked softly.

"What, darling?" he murmured sleepily.

"I'll give you a child."

"Yes." He drew her closer, like the most precious kind of treasure. Neither of them said "to replace the one you lost," but it was between them, all the same. She smiled, thinking about how it would be, the two of them and a little boy or a little girl to share their love with. Tears came to her eyes. I'll take care of him for you, Jessica, she said silently. And outside in the cool darkness, a nightbird began to sing.

Take 3 of
"The Best of the Best™"
Novels FREE
Plus get a FREE surprise gift!

Special Limited-time Offer

Mail to The Best of the Best™

3010 Walden Avenue
P.O. Box 1867
Buffalo, N.Y. 14269-1867

YES! Please send me 3 free novels and my free surprise gift. Then send me 3 of "The Best of the Best™" novels each month. I'll receive the best books by the world's hottest romance authors. Bill me at the low price of $3.99 each plus 25¢ delivery and applicable sales tax, if any.* That's the complete price and a savings of over 20% off the cover prices—quite a bargain! I understand that accepting the books and gift places me under no obligation ever to buy any books. I can always return a shipment and cancel at any time. Even if I never buy another book from Harlequin, the 3 free books and the surprise gift are mine to keep forever.

183 BPA A2P5

Name	(PLEASE PRINT)	
Address	Apt. No.	
City	State	Zip

This offer is limited to one order per household and not valid to current subscribers.
*Terms and prices are subject to change without notice. Sales tax applicable in N.Y.
All orders subject to approval.

Behind the iron lace gates of wealthy
New Orleans, beneath the veneer of her society
name, linger truths that Aurore Gerritsen has
hidden for a lifetime—truths that could change
forever the lives of her unsuspecting family.

EMILIE
RICHARDS

Invites you to meet the family hiding behind the gates of

IRON
Lace

Available this June, at your favorite retail outlet.

Bestselling Author

Invites you to play a deadly game of

The killer has struck twice already. Abigail Dean is
to be his final victim, taking to her grave a secret she
doesn't even know she possesses. Realizing that her
life's in danger, Abigail turns to Steve Kramer, a
man she believes she can trust. Now the killer must
silence two instead of one. And by working so
closely together, Abigail and Steve have become
an easy target.

Find out how it all ends, this June at your favorite
retail outlet.

If you love the romantic tales of

DIANA PALMER

Order now to receive more heartwarming stories
from this bestselling author: